BEYOND THE LAW

BEYOND THE LAW

J. ALLAN DUNN

ILLUSTRATED BY
ROGER B. MORRISON

COVER BY
GEORGE W. GAGE

POPULAR PUBLICATIONS · 2022

TABLE OF CONTENTS

BEYOND THE LAW

Himself hunted by the law, "Paul Standing"
daringly pits himself against gangland's
strongest and best-protected mob

1

SIGHTING THE QUARRY

I AM BEYOND the law.

That energetic and somewhat vindictive person, the district attorney, together with the judiciary, the police force, and all the organization gathered to prosecute the criminal and dispense the law—if not always justice—may not agree with me. To them I am a fugitive, an escaped convict, an outlaw; and they believe that sooner or later their dragnet will gather me in once more and return Richard Pemberton to a cell in Sing Sing. They are mistaken.

There is no Richard Pemberton. He has vanished into thin air, dissolved. As a matter of fact, there never was any one rightfully of that name. The one I have taken is of my own choosing. My own I never knew. When Harvey Pemberton adopted me he gave me his surname.

To use the colorful expression of a friend of mine, still behind the bars, a criminal, but a man of parts with much good in him that is now being rapidly atrophied by penitentiary life: they have no more chance of recovering the body of No. 6439, under which I was set down in the prison records, than of seeing rainbows in hell.

I am not railing, let it be understood in the beginning, against penitentiaries. I believe the system might be improved, but there are men there who should not be at liberty. There are some men I hope to see there. And there are, caged in such institutions, where the atmosphere is thick with the leaven of evil, of despair and fierce resentment, others who are innocent.

Not many men get away from Ossining Penitentiary beside the Hudson River. Yet it is not impossible for one who has money and friends—the right kind of friends. I had both. Still have them. And certain enemies.

And I am free. Free forever from the contaminating influence of the Big House that weakens a man's will and rots his soul, leaves him in the end less than a man, no better than a trapped animal. Free from the furtive eyes, the stealthy whisperings from mouth corners, the petty plots of miscalled trusties, the engendered hate that permeates the place where crime still breeds, where drugs enter, and the spirit of the underworld rules. Free from the stillness, the shadow of the bars that eats in, through to the heart, the rank smell of sweat and excrement.

A penitentiary! God save the word! He has little enough to do with the place.

Now—exit Richard Pemberton, Convict 6439, sentenced to ten years for felony. Enter Paul Standing, twenty-seven in actual years, white, sound of mind and body, at liberty.

It is not wise to give all the particulars of my escape. It would involve others who, whether they were bribed or acted from friendship, carried out their compacts faithfully. The law is still the law, though sometimes, to obtain justice, one must take it into his own hands. Besides its abuses, it has its uses. Politics and perjury are its maggots, breeding on bribery. But for the benefit of the authorities, lest those

Before they got through, they killed the old man

best restrained in the defense of decency and civilization
might discover it, as I did, I will mention the aqueduct that
runs through Ossining toward the city. It has places where
one may go in and out freely. It is a corridor to freedom.

When I came out of it there was a car waiting, not
conspicuously, but as it had waited for three nights,
parked each time at a different place, prearranged. It rolled
smoothly and not too fast toward New York. I was on the
floor for a time.

The driver was liveried, a typical chauffeur driving an
expensive, well-kept model. The only visible passenger
was a woman whose face, dress, and manner disarmed
suspicion. The bravest woman and comrade in the world.
Not mine, save as a friend, and never to be mine—I have
no right to dream of such a thing. But my friend always.

Presently the car swung off the main highway, sure it was
not followed, making surer. There had been no alarm. The
stuffed dummy in the cell was still No. 6439 to the auto-

matic inspection of the warder patrol. There were hours ahead of me—hours in which much must be done.

DISGUISE IS NOT a hard matter to one with intelligence and imagination. There were clothes in the car, make-up materials, an expensive wig that fitted well over cropped hair. The change was made in the grounds of a house known to both of us, closed for the late fall and winter.

Even if it had been noised abroad that Richard Pemberton had escaped, if the dicks were watching in New York, none of them, trained but limited as they are, would have connected him with the man in dinner clothes, dark of hair, tanned, erect and confident, escorting a woman of undoubted social standing, entering the select portals of the After Dark Club, whose members were elective and not casual, whose discreet entertainment had never been padlocked.

It was the woman whom the careful but courteous door-man admitted deferentially, merely glancing at her escort. She held the right of entry. Music played softly. Not every number was a dance. The dance floor was not a strip of parquetry where couples jostled each other to blatant jazz; it was at the back, cleverly lighted, tastefully decorated. There was nothing bizarre about the "After Dark." Its patrons drank vintages, not alleged whisky. They leisurely sipped their cordials.

In the *salle-à-manger*, tapestried, set with palms, with real flowers on the nooked tables, wagons were wheeled up by deft waiters while a *maitre d'hôtel* asked, and saw, if all was well. An exclusive, expensive place where our entrance was politely noticed, then ignored. They were playing something modern, of Debussy. I ordered with gusto. Viands and wines like these had long—too long—been strangers to me. I was hungry, and we ate as if we had no other purpose than to spend a pleasant hour or so.

Presently we danced. Prison drill had not made me clumsy, and to dance with Kate Wetherill would be inspiration to a buffoon. I had not yet seen the man I wanted. He was almost certain to arrive, and I could wait, though my blood tingled at the thought of meeting him.

He was the first on my list—the roster of men who had killed Harvey Pemberton, my benefactor and foster-father. He had been a man with a warp in his tapestry of life, but kindly, generous to all men save a certain vicious circle. Not all of them did I know, but I meant to find out.

It was for that I had escaped, had planned through the long nights—to uncover them, to deal out justice to them, to revenge the death of the best man I ever knew or hope to know, even as Kate was the best woman.

They had framed me, too—almost sent me to be burned in the Chair for what they had done. That was a lesser matter, though I was resolved to even the full score. There was one, chief in craft and cruelty, who had ordered this thing. But John Redding, bond broker, man about town, was to be the first victim. He was to be the wedge with which I would thrust to the secret of their racket, their identity.

It is a story that will unfold itself with this tale of mine, but some of it must be told now. I hold no brief against the world for Harvey Pemberton. I loved him, with cause. A faultless man is not lovable, by man or woman. He was the victim of unscrupulous speculators who ruined his fortune and his life and helped to send his wife to the grave, grieving not so much for their losses as the change in him. For Harvey Pemberton turned wolf. Part of him. The canker did not, could not, spoil his inherent sweetness.

HE DEVOTED HIS brain and energy to spoiling the spoilers. He preyed upon them, robbed them, if you will—using any and every method to take from them the gains they swindled the public out of with their schemes. He set himself outside the law. We lived in luxury. He picked me up, out of the streets, almost—friendless, parentless, penniless, a toss-up between the drudge I was and the crook I would probably have ultimately become.

It is environment that counts. Blood and breeding, if I ever possessed those in any real quality, are soon leached out by hunger and wretchedness. Brains, untrained, are transformed to nimble wits. One must live. Villon, the poet, was a vagabond.

But Pemberton took me, educated me, because he could not hate all as he prided himself he did. I knew nothing of his enterprises while I went, carefree but not without gratitude, through school and college. I saw his inner side. He made a man of me, training mind and body. It was not until I was twenty that I learned gradually what he was doing, whence came his wealth. He was growing old then, tired, but he was in a web of his own weaving that he kept me scrupulously out of.

"I have taken the wrong way," he told me, "and I am set upon it. But it is not for you to follow."

But I would not keep out of his trouble. He had been forced to form associations that he grew to hate but could not get rid of. Wolves of the underworld, racketeers, swin-

dlers, fences, thieves, he was with them but not of the pack.
His was only a wolfskin, after all.

There was no honor among them. Snarling or smil-
ing suspicion, according to their subtlety. Some hated, all
envied him, sneered at his insistence that I keep clear in
act if not in knowledge. There was a ring he grew to fear,
though he never showed it. They feared him, since there
were plots of theirs he knew about but would not enter
into. He never told who they were, but I was not a fool and
I knew that Redding, smooth, facile, insincere and a born
rogue and trickster, was one of them.

In the end they killed him. I came home to find him
dead, the modern wall-safe open, robbed. There was a gun
on the floor, one cartridge discharged. Mine! I carried it
to protect him, a flat automatic of foreign make, unmistakable, proved to belong to me. There were no clews, no
finger-prints. My hands were still gloved when they broke
in and took me.

Knowing him dead and unable to strike back, they had
laid information against him—and me. I had threatened
his life, they swore, had robbed and murdered the man who
had befriended me.

For that I had an alibi I could not use. I had been with
Kate. I could not resist the glory of her friendship, though
I knew, even before that, I could hope for nothing else. She
knew something of my life, exonerated me, saw the good
in Pemberton. True as a tempered, tested blade was Kate!
They knew of that alibi.

It was not necessary. I had others. A store where I had
bought cigarettes, a traffic officer I had spoken with. They
could not connect me with the time of his death. But he

was unmasked, his memory disgraced. The district attorney, fierce at losing a man he had been long seeking in vain, launched damaging invective against me, who had lived with him, been his close companion. If I had not killed him it was inconceivable that I had not been his accomplice. There were times when I had been with him when crime was committed. That was almost true. I had driven him, met him, guarded him, with knowledge that he was bent on affairs the law called criminal. One must not rob rascals.

The jury believed him, in full measure. I was *particeps criminis.* And so I became No. 6439, with the spirit of vendetta growing fiercer within me for every hour I spent in Sing Sing, growing more bitter and resolved. I was wealthy. Pemberton had set aside funds for me that could not be touched by the law.

Luck, or Fate, if there is such power outside a man, had worked for me while I was in the penitentiary. Certain holdings in oil and motor stocks had soared almost beyond belief. The source from which they had been bought was murky, but I dedicated my riches to the one end.

I could not clear my foster-father's name. It was hallowed only to me, who knew the real man. But I could take vengeance. And now the time had come.

THEY HAD TAKEN that gun of mine. It belonged now to the State. It is curious how a thing of metal, a weapon, will become a fetish to a man bent upon using it in reprisal. I could get another, but I had often wished for that one— never as much as now, with Redding coming into the After Dark, a blond beauty with him, dressed in the extreme mode, too well dressed, her languid air affected, sleek as a

Persian kitten, probably as greedy and selfish. She amused
Redding for the moment, and he served her narrow ends.

A pulse throbbed in my throat; veins corded on my forehead. My elaborate plans dissolved in hatred, in the desire
to come to hand grips with the debonair scoundrel. I felt
Kate's light, firm grip on my arm, and at once got hold of
myself. Redding was but to be bait for the rest. We went
back to our table.

I gave Kate a cigarette, lit it for her, one for myself, with
a steady hand. My nerves were under control. The hot rage
had changed to cold calculation.

"It is he?" she said lightly, with a smile, as if she had
jested.

"One of them," I answered. "The first, but not the last."

"I knew it by your eyes," she said. "They were—terrible.
I was afraid of you for a moment."

"Not now?" I asked.

Her smile was unforced as she shook her head.

"Not then, really. But I should be if I thought you looked
that way at me. He does not seem very dangerous," she
added, for as the tables were arranged there was no fear
of our being overheard. "Vain, selfish, and in some ways
weak."

"It's not what he is," I said. "He has the protection of
the rest of his crowd and the hired racketeers."

"Gunmen?"

I nodded. She understood what a gunman was, these
days. A bravo who tried to look like a gentleman, who
wore thirty-dollar silk shirts, aspired to elegance. There
were some of them now in the After Dark, sitting quietly
enough, inconspicuous, a trifle ill at ease for all their calling.

They were paid for the club's protection by an interest in the profits. Aside from that, they had other regular income. Their mob might stick up a pay roll, but they were more likely to be employed breaking strikes. They were vicious enough, and in their own wars utterly ruthless. A world of their own within the underworld.

"What are you going to do?" she asked me.

"Nothing—here. I shall follow him when he leaves. I do not know where he lives. Then I am going to ask him a few questions—and he is going to answer them."

"He will not recognize you. Nobody would," she said. "But suppose we go now? We can wait in my car until they come out, then trail them."

"You are keeping out of this." I spoke harshly, keyed up.

"You can't keep me out entirely, Dick."

"Paul! Paul Standing, from now on. You may not know me next time you do see me. Disguises are tricky. They are only applied. You can drive me if you will. I'll leave you as soon as I've got him located."

I knew it was useless to argue with her, as I knew, deep within me, she would always know me, however changed. There were things between us, an affinity of friendship that should never have been allowed, would not have been if I had been less of a boy when I first knew her. It was as natural as the tuning-in of certain vibrations, the leap of electricity between poles.

It would not be wise to take a cab. They were too easily traced. I did not know what might happen, save that I would get through to Redding. And Ben Donlin, Kate's chauffeur, was absolutely to be trusted.

Redding was dancing with his blonde when we rose.

She seemed to be pouting about something. I fancied they might be leaving soon. We got our outer clothes, and the doorman called the car. Kate ordered Ben to drive around the block and park across the street, where we could watch the entrance.

The After Dark was on a side thoroughfare, a quiet "one-way," without much traffic at that time of night. The girl with Redding was the type who would spend several minutes assuring herself of her face value before she left or arrived anywhere.

KATE SLID HER hand into a side-pocket of the car, handed me the object she took from it, an automatic pistol.

"I got it for you," she said. "You may need it. Ben has one. I have a permit."

I slid the deadly thing into my hip pocket without a word. With us, words were not always needed.

She, like myself, had no relatives—at least, not in evidence. Her mother had died long ago. Her father had left her a fortune in her own right. She had friends in her own set, by right of birth, but she was independent. I had met her at a country club. She was a sportswoman, her splendid body vigorous and supple.

Her mind grasped readily any subject. Unlike most women, she did not limit herself to her emotions, nor consider them infallible instincts. Those she had, swift and unerring intuitions, but she reasoned matters out. None like her. None.

Something kept her from any definite plan of life, from marriage or a career, eminently capable as she was. Her friendships were sacred things. For me she had done much, risked more than I dreamed of, though in the penitentiary

I was powerless to prevent her entering the plans for my escape and making them successful. I could not persuade her to break with me. Some day it would have to be done— when I was through with my grim mission. Not now!

"I wish I could go with you," she said. "It's getting into my blood, Paul."

There was something else getting into mine that I fought hard against. The desire to say things I should infinitely regret, to cross the line I had set up between us never to be crossed. It was sex, ruling the world, that sent my pulses up and made me twitch my lighter for cigarettes, forcing my face to a mask as I revealed it. The gun made itself felt in my pocket. It fitted loosely and would come out fast, though a hip pocket is a foolish place to carry one.

There are those who say that a man can draw swifter from a holster at his hip than from a spring-clip shoul-der-clutch. That depends upon the man. Equal practice, equal coordination, will give little to choose between the two. And in New York, where arms are forbidden, the citizen and every cheap crook packs one, the advantages of concealment are obvious. Kate leaned forward a little with a light gasp.

"There they are," she whispered. "Follow them, Ben."

It was the woman's car, I decided, not a man's type of motor. The driver was colored. They drove east, to Fifth Avenue, and then down town. We trailed them without trouble.

I have often wondered what blood ran in my veins. Hot blood somewhere. Hot bursts of impulse balanced almost instantly by restraint, automatic, the result of one of those mixed strains that, like Scotch-Irish, carry a man far on sudden urges and then steady him, get him out of it. Perhaps mine was that mixture. I did not know, will never know. But it has always seemed to me it was the man that counted, not the pedigree of the child.

That temperament of mine held me now cool as shadow-ice, unusually alert, charged with an energy that stored itself up, ready for action. My mind was active, not considering what to do, but confident that it would click when that time came. It was coming—fast.

They turned east again, beyond Park Avenue, then south. The car stopped by a small apartment building remodeled from three old-time brownstone houses. On one side of it there was a low fence of boards, beyond that a great excavation. A big theater was in the course of construction, by the sign. The foundations had been put in, and then something had been found wrong with the plans, the work had stopped for reorganization. It formed an irregular L from the middle of one block to that of another, on the side street. Its space backed the apartment building and I surveyed it with satisfaction.

We saw Redding get out, lift his hat with a mocking air, enter the narrow lobby. We drove past the car and saw the blonde, her face sulky, powdering her nose. She had not yet given her order to go on. I made Kate let me out two blocks away.

"I'm telling Ben to drive you straight home," I said. "Good night."

"Good night," she answered. "And—good luck, Paul."

I was likely to need it. Redding, if he was weak, was the more likely to have taken adequate means of not being caught by surprise. He walked on a narrow plank, and he knew it. Kate had never sought to dissuade me from my purpose. She knew its hazards, and all her upbringing was against it, but I fancied that in her heart she approved. Even as, God knows why, she approved of me.

2

DRAWN GUNS

GETTING IN WAS not too much of a problem. I am not
a burglar, a peterman, or a second-story man, but I have
friends in all those lines—and others. Nefarious gentry, no
doubt, but to be trusted by those they liked. My friends
were not of the vicious circle of Redding, not vultures but
hawks of hazard, simpler, making small pretense, proud of
their misused abilities.

I could have got a lock picked or a key made for any
purpose. They liked me because of my foster-father. Somehow they respected his keeping me out of crookdom. They
used to call me the Kid. I had messages from them in the
penitentiary, transmitted by prison methods. They had
helped me already, would do it again. And I might have to
call on them before I got through.

Now it was easy. There was a drowsy negro who answered
the door, the telephone and the elevator on the night-shift.
He opened to me.

"Redding home yet?" I asked.

"Yessa."

"Take me up."

His eyes rolled. "Can't do that, boss. Mistuh Redding,
he done give orders not to—"

"I know all about that," I said. "I'm different. I saw him this evening at the After Dark, but couldn't speak to him. He wasn't alone. But I've got to see him. It's important."

He saw the orange back of a bill in my hand, and he was vanquished, with that and my evident knowledge of Redding's ways. But he was still doubtful as the elevator stopped on the third floor, wider awake. He would know me again. But not the man I would be before many hours were past.

"You know which 'partment, boss?"

"Sure."

That reassured him, and I stopped to light a cigarette. I had taken another look at that excavation when I came back. There was a watchman on the side street, in front of a taller hoarding, under a platform—an old man, useless, given the perfunctory job out of pull or pity, fast asleep and snoring in a tilted chair. There was nothing to steal. The contractors had struck a spring, and a pipe lay like a great serpent sucking up the flow, its pump pulsing automatically.

But I had seen more than this: lights on the third floor, at the rear, that had not been there when we drove past. I knew the general layout of such places. Redding would do himself well in his bachelor quarters, where ladies were not unknown. He might have a servant.

At that he had his name on the door frame in a silver holder. I touched the bell. A Japanese stood there with searching, beady eyes, hostile. Something else came into them as I thrust the muzzle of the gun against his livery vest he wore under the service Tuxedo jacket. He backed up, discreetly silent, his brown face turning to yellow. He, too, had seen something in my eyes.

"Get out," I said, talking like an ex-convict out of the corner of my lips, soundless, but audible to his senses. "And stay out! If you come back—" I ended that sentence and punctuated it with a little thrust of the gun. He had seen men talk like that before, knew their habits. He was not Redding's picked man for nothing.

I watched him go and softly slid a bolt. It might not prove entirely adequate, but I was inside—and so was Redding.

He was humming to himself, mixing a highball. He had put on a handsome—too handsome—brocaded dressing gown. For a moment I looked at him as he was, sensuous, self-satisfied, marked by self-indulgence, a little bald, a little too fat and flabby, pouches indicated under his eyes. I had made no sound. I had put away the gun. There were other ways of managing a man like him. I might need it presently.

"Who the devil are you, and how did you get in?" he demanded imperiously, but he was upset, nervous, frightened.

"You named me," I told him. "The very devil himself, Redding, as far as you are concerned. But I can take a drink."

I did not want it, did not mean to drink with him, but it gave him time to pull himself together. I had given him a fright, it was plain. I wanted a business talk with him, and intended to be clearly understood.

"I sent your man away," I told him. "We are going to have a chat. I've come some distance under some difficulty,

to talk with you, Redding. It is very much to your interest
to listen, and reply."

I GUESSED THEN that he was a traitor to his own. He lived
in dread of being found out. But he breathed more easily,
his nostrils were no longer dinted by the fingermarks of
terror. Some confidence came back to him as he drained
his glass, rudely enough, poured out another tot and passed
the decanter to me, indicating the siphon and silver bowl
of ice, handing me a tall tumbler. I was to find out later
what had restored him.

I marked the change then and did not like it, but time
was passing. Daylight was not far away, and I had to get
out before it arrived.

I took a seat and he another, in a lounging chair. The
room was a semi-studio, with a fireplace and a balcony,
paneled, well-furnished, though with more of the bric-
a-brac trifles called *bibelots* than most men would like. It
was heated, but the night was warm and a window was
open, screened against insects and draped with a blind
three-quarters down, moving a little in the light breeze. I
caught sight of a fire escape, prescribed by building regu-
lations.

"If it's anything about bonds," he said. "I assume no
responsibility beyond preliminary advice. I don't know
how you got in—"

"And you don't know how I got *out*," I said. "It has
something to do with bonds, Redding, but not the sort
you peddle."

His nose looked pinched again. Apprehension was
giving him a hunch. His eyes bulged and he started

forward, to fall back as I took off the wig. My hair is blond and the prison bristles must have glittered under the light.

"Good God!" he said, and sat rigid. A fine right he had to be invoking the Deity!

I had underestimated him a little. It was a mistake. He was proving stubborn, after the first shock. I had watched him closely, thinking he might be fool enough to try to give an alarm, and I fancied he had contrived some sort of signal. He was almost at his ease.

"You've been brooding over things," he said. "A jail is a morbid sort of place, I imagine. If you were innocent I can understand your attitude. But it did look bad for you on the face of it. You've been threatening me, Pemberton, and no man likes to be threatened. I'll overlook that. I had nothing to do with the affair. It's ridiculous to assume such a thing. There is no ring. I was a friend of your foster-father."

"That's a lie," I said flatly. "Redding, you look like the sharks you travel with, but you're only a dogfish. Small fry. That is why my threats, as you call them, but which are really promises, stopped where they did. I say again that I'll let you off if you come clean. But don't lie to me. When you say you were not mixed up with the killing and robbery of Harvey Pemberton, you lie, out of your yellow instinct to dodge. Very definite information came to me concerning that. Plenty of news seeps into Sing Sing, Redding. It's condensed and limited, but it's true. I *know* you were there. That came from a man who used to work for your racket once, did then. He's marking time in a prison laundry now. With a strong idea that your mob put him there."

That hit him. I could see his memory working. He realized I was in earnest. Yet something bolstered him.

I watched him narrowly. His right hand and arm hung loosely over the padded arm of his chair. He was up to something, if it was not already accomplished.

"DID YOU EVER consider a door, Pemberton?" he asked. "You never know what may enter through a door. It holds the element of the unexpected. Men or women, coming in unannounced. Much may come in through a door. Hope, despair, joy, sorrow, life or death."

"A sweetheart or the sheriff," I broke in. I was getting tired of the waste of time. I believed he was trying to divert my attention. His hand was on the arm now and he let it drop to his side. There must be a gun snuggled down between the cushions. I was sure of it.

"Did you ever think of windows in the same relation?" I asked him, playing his own game. "Especially windows with fire escapes outside."

I risked a side glance myself as the blind shifted again. It might be the wind, but I thought I saw some movement behind the screen that, in turn, might be only the shadow of the flapping blind on the wire. Redding did not move.

"We were talking of doors, Pemberton."

His eyes were glittering with a triumph he could no longer suppress. He had pulled some trick. I went for my gun.

"You'll talk, damn you!" I told him. "Or you'll go out." I meant it. Then I froze. There was a long Venetian mirror, displayed on an elaborate priest robe. In it I saw a section of paneling back of me that had pivoted. A man was stepping through, short, silent, sinister, his features like a carving, a mask of malice. I knew that face, knew what was behind those pale eyes—the lust to kill.

It was "Fin" Murray, gangster, gunman! He had been at the After Dark. I knew his record. His left hand—his "fin"—had been crushed with the slamming of a car door in a hasty get-away, but he still made his living with his right. He must be protecting Redding's mob. His gun was trained on my spine. He could smash my vertebra with the quirk of his finger.

"Get this guy, Fin!" said Redding, his polite parlance turned to mob vernacular. "He talks too much. Knows too much."

I was looking at Fin's reflection, my own hand still on the butt of the gun I dared not draw. Every instant I expected to see his weapon's muzzle spit flame, to feel the swift paralysis of death. I would probably never hear the report with my spinal cord severed. And he held his fire. His voice was high, primed by cocaine.

"Where you goin' to dump him?" he demurred. Fin knew his trade, its advantages and its drawbacks. He was a professional. But Redding, never able to be more than amateur at anything, lost control, almost screaming.

"It's Pemberton, you fool! He's broken out from Sing Sing. To hell with his body! He's here to get a stake, see? Threatening. Bump him off."

I have been close to death lately, many times, never seemingly closer than then. But my faculties were clear. An automatic thought jumped up in my mind: "Here you go!" That was all. I've had others tell me the same thing, exploding the old idea about a flash back of all your past life. One has no time for that when waiting for a bullet from a gunman's rod.

Murray, of course, knew how I stood with his world.

Perhaps he held a certain respect for a man who had jumped the Big House. Whatever it was, he hesitated and then my heart leaped and I closed my eyes to hide what they might show.

THE REAL DOOR had opened, swiftly, and a woman glided in, to the right of Fin. She was in evening attire. Under the waving brown hair lace had been made into a mask to cover the upper part of her face. Her eyes gleamed through the screen. Her head was high, and her mouth and chin steady as the hand that held a gun as in a vise, held it on Fin, who held his on me. Here was a stalemate, a deadlock. Gangster *versus* highwaywoman. No doubt to me who she was. Kate With her chauffeur's gun. Her voice was disguised as she snapped out shrill command.

"Don't get funny, Fin! Drop the gat! *Drop it!* Now kick it over this way. You're all through."

He snarled, not at her, but at me.

"Your moll turns the card, this trick. Damn her!"

I forgave him that oath, even against Kate. It was tribute. And I was busy. It had not been a stalemate. Redding was still on the board. He had intended right along to kill me, I believe, as soon as he knew I was Pemberton. He had known Fin was on the way and had held composure until the last. Now he was in a frenzy of rage and hate. I saw him dive for the cushions of the chair, and I smashed his elbow with a slug from the gun I slid out easily enough now without Fin's rod covering me.

Redding dropped on one knee, crumpled into the chair, holding his arm while blood sopped through his sleeve and stained the cushions. His gun fell to the floor, and I stooped swiftly for it, an eye all the time on Fin and Kate. She had been magnificent, but she might relax and Murray, speeded up with cocaine, could move and strike like a snake, lithe as a lizard. But Kate had her small foot on the weapon he had kicked over to her. Her hand was still steady.

The roar of the heavy weapon she had given me in the car, the one yell from Redding, his collapse, the bright blood and the reek of powder gas did not upset her, though Fin was half crouching, poised like a lightweight boxer waiting for an opening.

I had to get her out of there, get away myself. The light back of the window screen was already graying. The house might be alarmed. It was the hour for janitors' visits for garbage pails. That shot of mine had sounded like a clap of thunder. There was the negro elevator boy, the Jap. I fancied Kate must have met the latter and got him to let her in. In that case—

The panel entrance was pivoting again. Again a short figure showed its reflection to me in the mirror. Short and squat and swarthy, slant of eye, the Japanese, with a knife balanced for the throw.

The steel blade came like an arrow as I ducked. It struck the Venetian mirror where my image had been, it smashed the glass, shattering, splintering it, with seven years' hard luck for somebody. Kate thought to see that knife buried between my shoulder blades. The gleaming passage of it hypnotized her for perhaps the twentieth of a second, the time it takes the human eye to function at top speed. It was enough for Fin to take his chance.

He dived at her, low, like a tackle taking out a man. Asaki, Redding's man, went into action at the same time. It was a triple play for the gun under Kate's foot. She went down before Fin's flying leap, her bullet passed over his head and slapped into the wall, but she sent the gunman's weapon sliding over the floor toward me. A rug checked it.

Asaki took a skip and a jump for it. He was almost on all fours as I knocked him out with the barrel of my own gun before I picked up Fin's, got Asaki's knife to insure safety, though the Jap was out with a gash in his scalp and more blood welling out of his black pompadour to spoil a fine rug.

Redding had not recovered from his nerve shock. Only the man who feels lead or steel on his bone knows what that is. It breaks down all coordination and the pain of his elbow must have been intense.

It was all as fast as first-class baseball. Faster. Kate was on her feet, active as a squirrel. They had both gone down together and she had been the quicker of the two. Fin's nose was bloody from a blow from her knee, one eye was going to be a shiner. She had fought him savagely for possession of her own gun, and his crippled left hand gave her the advantage, though I think she was a match for him, cocaine and all.

SHE WAS MAD now, clean through. Human enough, her eyes sparkling.

"You dirty little crook!" she cried. "How dare you touch me! If I killed you, you had it coming to you."

I almost laughed, for all the emergency. The lights were paling in the globes, the window was pink how, not gray. Those three shots must have roused the house. I knew how most of them would take it. New Yorkers are not prone to rush out where bullets fly. There are too many bystanders killed in these racketing times. But they would send in an alarm.

Yet the mixture of admiration and defiance on Fin's face was ludicrous. So was his defense.

"I ain't a crook, sister, I'm a gunman, and you had my rod. You're sure some scrappin' moll!"

Fancy Kate Wetherill's friends seeing her like this, called a "scrappin' moll!"

I caught her by the wrist and she tried to shake me off before she understood what she was doing—and I realized the temper she could show when she was provoked.

There should be another fire escape at the back. That assumption was a bit of a gamble; but the elevator was not to be thought of, and to take the stairs might mean running into the clutch of the law, summoned already and on its way. The fire escape off the room would expose us to the view of the street.

I almost forced Kate to the door and then she gave way to me, trusting herself. She was in a position as bad as my own. The elevator was downstairs. It would take an officer to persuade the negro to bring it up to this floor. The front apartment in this section of the house seemed unoccupied or untenanted. No one looked out at us as we made the window at the end of the hall, climbed through, closed it and went down the iron ladders.

I fancied that Fin made for the other window as we left. I was not sure, but thought he would not stay there with the Jap knocked out, and Redding in the shape he was. And he would not feel like trailing us. We had his gun. I was a perfect armory as I descended, with the guns and the knife in my pockets.

I swung down the last link of the ladder, dropped from its end, caught Kate as she jumped, raced with her across the excavation, over the low foundations and sneaked through a workman's gate to the street. The old watchman was still asleep. It was then I heard something like a shot, but it might have been a car muffler.

Kate had her mask off, she had her cloak on still, and I had coat and hat. We had left nothing behind. I had long since replaced the wig. A man and woman in evening dress at dawn are not necessarily conspicuous in Manhattan, but they stand out, are likely to be remembered. They would hardly have sent a posse from the station. If Redding had put in an alarm it would be different, but I did not think he felt much like anything but getting hold of a doctor.

STILL, IN A few minutes it would be known that Richard Pemberton had escaped from Sing Sing, that he was in disguise. They would be finding that dummy in the cell soon. I take no credit for it, but I was not thinking then about myself. Kate had to be cleared.

"Where did you leave the car?" I asked her. It was close by, thank fortune, and we made it without comment. There was not so many people on the streets. The cars were not running, the subways were not yet discharging their hordes of workers, and no cabs passed us as we sauntered on with blood tingling, urging us to run, fearing every moment to hear the whistle of a harness bull, the beat of running feet. But we made it and nobody stared at us. Ben started the motor and got the car rolling, sliding in easy gears. We were off, south this time, swinging to the avenue.

"I told Ben to take you straight home," I said, none too

gently. I was shaken now the emergency was past, panicky at the thought of what might have happened.

"He seemed to think it was my car," she answered. "Anyway, if I had not gone back—"

"I should have been dead and out of it. It would all be ended. You may be dragged into it yet." She laid her hand on mine and I thrilled under the warm, electric touch.

"I never enjoyed anything so much in my life," she said. And meant it. "Where shall I take you?"

I reflected, considered the risks, balanced them. There were other clothes for me, money, necessities at the apartment of a friend. It was not very far and it was best for me to go there in a private car, to get under cover as soon as possible. She knew where it was, but she was not sure what I wanted to do the way things were. She was standing by for orders and she should never have been in the same galley with me.

"You've done enough," I said. "Too much. When I leave you it has got to be good-by. That's final."

"It takes two to make a friendship, and two to break it," she answered. "Must you go on with this? What made you take the name of Paul? Why will you kick against the pricks?"

I knew my Bible well enough to understand the allusion.

"What else is there for me to live for?" I asked. I dare say I was bitter. "A nameless man, an ex-convict—"

"Unjustly that, Paul."

I would not be silenced. "One who has lived with the underworld. Not knowing who I am. What else is there?"

Her eyes seemed to give answer, but I dared not interpret their message. There was the sun of her spirit shining through rain. Hope through her tears. Twin rainbows in my individual hell!

3

THE PETERMAN

THERE IS A doctor, a surgeon whose name it would be folly to give. It is no more his own than mine is, but it is widely known. He got into some trouble that does not concern this story. He had done wonderful work in facial surgery during and after the war. Many a poor devil owes his human resemblance to Blessing's humanity. We'll call him Blessing.

When he was through with his mix-up he changed his State with his name, got a certificate, and now he lifts faces for women who feel young and want to look it. Men also. Vanity knows no sex. All sorts and conditions of people go to him and pay him an income that is almost fabulous. A lot of night club and theatrical folk. He does not ask them where their money comes from. But he would do much for nothing if it was needed, has done it, for the halt and the maimed.

He knew all about me. I don't know if he believed in me or not. I think he did. He consented to make a new Paul Standing out of the old Richard Pemberton. I had an appointment with him. And I had a new wig to keep it in, blond this time, to wear until my prison crop grew out.

He was going to do things to my hair also. Blessing was a supreme artist.

The apartment was complete and comfortable. I had seen no one as I came in with my own latchkey. My friend had gone to Long Island to make room for me. He owned a small place there, near the shore, and I was going there later. I did not know what scars I might have to heal from Blessing's surgery. I had no others on my body, then, no distinguishing marks.

It would be November, perhaps, before I could come back. All that length of marking time. I had failed, so far, with Redding. But I did not worry about that. I would lay better plans next time. I had been too eager to commence, to get names and lay my schemes while my face got into its new shape. I might commute for awhile, until plans matured. But, if I came back to New York, or not, I was going to stay out of Kate Wetherill's way—for both our sakes.

I proposed wearing a different type of clothes, cultivating a change of gait, affecting certain mannerisms. These things, needed for my new identity, would prevent her recognizing me, unless we stood face to face. That must be avoided. She must not tread my path, for it would be perilous enough, I realized, and might well end in disaster. She must not be embroiled.

My appointment with Blessing was for one o'clock. I slept soundly, awoke to the bell of the alarm I had set, strange for a moment in my new surroundings. It was a treat to bathe, to shave luxuriously, renew my artificial tan, don clean linen and the new clothes. I hardly recognized my own image in the door-length mirror of the bathroom.

The suit was sporty. The wig changed me. I looked like a chap who lived much out of doors, playing golf and tennis, swimming and boating—not in the least like an escaped convict.

I walked leisurely to a near-by and excellent restaurant. There would be no news in the morning papers, I reflected, though I meant to buy one. They had all gone to press before I prodded Asaki out of my way with the gun. It was quite possible that Redding would hush things up. He would get in touch with his crowd and they had ways of smothering things. There would be nothing, unless some early or ultra-late bird of a reporter got word of the alarm from a desk sergeant.

That was hardly likely. By the time the afternoon papers were ready Redding's people would have muzzled the police. It was only a fracas; after all, unless they decided to denounce me. They might prefer to get me themselves, make sure I was out of the way for keeps this time, give me a ride or set their gangsters on me.

It was purely business with those gunmen. I felt sure that Fin felt little rancor. He was more likely to be envying me my "scrappin' moll." He was far from the truth, but she had certainly acted the role, consciously or unconsciously. To-day I do not know which.

But the afternoon papers would have the news of my escape. The tabloids would eat it up.

I bought a morning paper and, as I paid for it, a van dashed up and a lad delivered a bundle of papers to the corner stand. They were tabloids, the front page pictured, heavy type.

"Extry!" said the deliverer. "Big sale, Bud. Murder, an' a guy got out of Sing Sing to do it!"

IT WAS A tribute to the quality of my nerves that I showed no eager interest. I saw Redding's name and my own— Pemberton. I saw his portrait staring up at me, next to mine. Whoever might have been my parents, they had given me a sound body, good fibers. I turned the paper over and only bought it as the vendor thrust it at me. And I tucked it inside my morning sheet and walked down the street, sure that if they were trying to find me from that halftone engraving, they were going to have a hard time of it. And wait till Blessing got through with me!

The hunt was up, the hounds were baying, trying to get a strong lead. They had got the scent at Redding's. Now that the game was in play I felt a strong sense of elation. I was like a dog-fox who knows his speed, knows he has earth to run to when he is tired of the chase that he enjoys.

I ordered well. Honeydew melon, eggs Benedict, buttered toast, coffee. Not much like prison fare. And it was not until I had broken my first egg yolk that I glanced, first at the morning paper, turning to the sports page, then, fastidiously, at the tabloid sheet. I was playing a part. I had the thrill of the actor.

I held no idea that I had killed Redding. Even if blood-poisoning sets in, a man does not die from a shattered elbow in a few hours. Somebody had done it. Not Asaki. He was out of the question. Fin could have, if Redding blamed him, as he might, for the mess he had made of it, outwitted by a scrappin' moll.

But I did not think so. I had a hunch, remembering the shadow on the wire screen. Remembering Redding's fear at my entrance and another hunch that I had held. If his mob thought he had talked they would see to it promptly that he talked no more. Or double-crossed them. He was just the sort of fatuous fool who thought his wits were equal to those of the men who actually planned their coups.

The police did not know. They were in a rare coil. It was the inspiration of a newsman, an editor, far sharper than any Central Office dick, who tied up my name with the identity of the murderer. They had done that more from a publicity standpoint than otherwise.

Here was the story. An alarm had been sent in. An officer had answered it, ringing for reserves when he saw what had happened. Asaki still out, a shattered mirror, Redding dead, with a bullet in his brain. They thought he had been shot twice, but the bullet in his arm did not match that in his brain. The autopsy had been swift. Murder is something that spurs speed with police and press.

The only weapon found was one fully loaded between the blood-stained cushions of the chair, from which Redding had evidently pitched forward, the arm soaked with gore. They had missed, as yet, the fact that it had taken time for that blood to soak in. The best of detectives got excited in the beginning. And it was rather a fine point.

The Jap told what he said he knew, when they revived him. There was no mention of the knife. The shattered mirror was still a mystery. And Fin was out of it. I guessed what he had done—gone up to the roof and made his get-away unnoticed. The wily Oriental resorted to Eastern silence.

"A man had come, thrusting a gun at him, shoving him outside. Later, a woman. She wore a mask. A friend of Mr.

Redding's was there when she arrived. He did not know his name, only that he came there often. And he was tall and thin."

I blessed the Oriental's idea. Fin, tall and thin! Asaki was not going to get mixed up in any Occidental trouble, held as a witness, browbeaten. In the lingo of the day, he knew his apples. His world was limited to his own ambitions and they did not include notoriety.

Yet he described me fairly well, as I had appeared. He was vaguer about Kate. I had quarreled with Redding. Redding's tall, thin friend had interfered. Asaki had come in and been hit over the head. That was all he knew about it. He had seen no gunplay, except that he might have been hit with a gun. It had all happened too swiftly for him to be sure.

Evasive Asaki! I was willing to pay his fare home to Tokyo, or wherever he hailed from, and give him a thousand dollars to boot, though I knew he was only playing 'possum to save bother.

BUT THE EDITOR linked up the two big news breaks that had come his way. He knew what his public wanted. Sensation! He had all the elements of a fictionist, save the power of generating his own plots and the technique of magazine writing. But when the actual materials were at hand he worked fast enough.

He harked back to my trial, to the tragedy of Harvey Pemberton. He had more than news sense, that man—a hunch, inspired, doubtless, by his desire to make a crashing story. He found enough to color the supposition. It was true that the "man" did not resemble Richard Pemberton, but—here he landed on the truth—Pemberton would have had time to get from Sing Sing, since the warden could not say how long after the cell doors had been closed it was that Pemberton had escaped. Evidently he had disguised himself, being a clever individual whose college career had shown imagination, besides physical prowess.

During his trial, the story continued, young Pemberton's lawyer had sought to show that his client had never been associated with any of his foster-father's affairs. He had called witnesses, Redding among them. And Redding had disclaimed any knowledge at all of the matter. He had, he testified, sold Harvey Pemberton various securities, but he knew nothing as to the source of his income, was not interested. His evidence had been damaging rather than helpful. Under cross-examination by the prosecution Redding had managed to leave a suggestion that the prisoner handled much of his benefactor's business and not too satisfactorily.

From there on he was cagy, that tabloid editor, scenting libel. But he insinuated there might have been bad blood between Redding and Richard Pemberton. It was really very cleverly done. He made a problem of it, a query that his readers would delight in.

In point of fact it was the attitude of Redding at my trial, his deliberate attempt to decry me, that had crystallized my own suspicions of him. He managed to be convincing, if not sincere in anything but the determination to help to make a scapegoat out of me.

Now one thing stood out very clearly. I could not keep my appointment with Blessing. I must get to Redding's rooms and ransack them. He had been my only lead. Remembering his trick door I could well imagine that he had some hiding place where he would stow papers away. He was just the kind who would hold incriminating records that should be destroyed, to protect himself against his own associates, to use in self-defense, or in accusation of them if he considered it needful.

I had got several sidelights on Redding, tips while in the penitentiary. He would double-cross his best friend, a modern Judas. And now he was nothing. It was my hunch that his own mob had bumped him off as dangerous and unnecessary. It was only coincidence—or fate, if you like— that had taken me to his apartments on the same night. Now I had to go back there without delay. The hunch whispered it, shouted it in my brain.

Hunches are curious things. Most people ignorantly connect them with superstition. But they are based, I have found, upon definite enough matters; things learned by instinctive observation, facts tucked away for future reference, the deductions of experience, all working in the subconscious—part of the automatic machinery of our life; suddenly arriving in the conscious and announcing itself.

It announced now, very definitely, that if I did not get through to whatever information Redding had tucked away, some one else would. The man who killed him had been held off from his chance until the last minute. He had had to beat it as the rest of us had done—and I believed that he went up and over the roofs, well ahead of Fin. If he had had time he would have searched as he had been ordered.

They would send again. During the day the place would be visited by the police, the press writers and photographers, the morbid and the merely curious. They would wait until nightfall, for the quiet hours when people out ordi-

narily late to theater and supper are home, and the roister-
ers just commencing their night club rounds. So would I.

I FINISHED MY breakfast, left the papers as if they were
of little moment and went to a cigar store to find a public
phone. I called up Blessing, who understood and post-
poned my making-over. I walked on to another pay-station
and called another number. It was over in the once famous
Bowery district.

I had to repeat a pass-phrase before they would acknowledge they knew Mother Sara Levinsky. Then she came to
the phone wanting to know who it was.

"It's the Kid." I had to tell her that and I could hear her
wheeze and gasp. She knew I was out, of course, but she
seemed glad to hear my voice.

"I want to see Billings," I said. "It's business and it's
urgent."

"You vaid a minnid," she said. It was nearer five. I had to
feed the machine nickels before she came back.

"Ad six o'clock, in Washington Square."

"Fine!" I rang off, contented. I had to have an expert on
this job and Billings was the man. He was a cockney, born
in Hackney, London. He had a little shop south of Washington Square where he officially made keys, mended locks
and handles. He called himself a tinker and he was a genius
in his way. Given education and better opportunity, eliminate the unmoral quirk in his system which, plus a certain
love of adventure, made him what he was, and he could
have gone far, according to my foster-father. But he was
like the expert fisherman or hunter who would rather
poach than establish an honest reputation.

Billings had a safety device for vaults and safes. He was

always perfecting it and then inventing means to spoil his
own craft. He could have patented and sold for a fortune—
but there it was, the twist that has something of vanity in
it, that makes a man like to prove himself smarter than his
smug fellows.

You didn't often find Billings in his shop. He used to
go out for bluefish, watch a baseball game, he even played
bowls with the enthusiasts at Central Park, his bulldog
guarding his coat. An outdoors man, in the daytime. But,
when night came and the occasion was ripe, Billings would
listen to the click of falling tumblers, bore through invinci-
ble steel with oxy-acetylene, set levers to wrench off doors
or, perhaps—though he did not like the method—make
little cups of soap, fill them with "soup," cover with blan-
kets and blow a safe.

He was a king peterman, Billings. What he didn't know
about safes was not worth bothering about. A good, solid,
dependable sort, if he liked you, crook though he was. He
never tied up with any mob, but was called in as an expert:
that was Billings. I felt a whole lot better now that I had
the probability of getting him to come along with me. I
was not even an amateur.

I read all the editions as they came out, buying one here,
one there. Men have been nailed for showing too much
interest in papers. My disguise was good, but it was only
temporary. Arrest would land me back in a hurry no matter
on what suspicion they took me in. That wig was a certain
give-away.

It was Kate I was worried about. Another tabloid had
taken up the theory of the Mystery Woman. Asaki had
been grilled again without result. They might as well have

questioned the Big Buddha at Kamakura. But the paper proceeded on the French theory of *cherchez la femme*—which isn't by any means exclusively French. All dicks seek the woman, and watch her. Often enough she gets jealous and gives her man away. Almost invariably the escaping prisoner turns up where his moll is waiting, with the dicks in the offing. They use the lure of sex to supplement their own deficiencies.

But they could not establish the identity of the masked woman. It had been a close shave, there must not be any more such; but they did not know where to lurk for Convict 6439. Not all the papers subscribed to the idea that I was the man who had killed Redding. It was generally printed as an "it is suggested" item. And the police were saying little. Neither was the warden. They all expected to have me inside of twenty-four hours. The warden thought I was still hiding inside the penitentiary walls, and pooh-poohed the murder idea. The pack was at fault, but they would not acknowledge it. Meantime, the smart tabloid editor had got very warm.

NONE OF THEM dreamed that I would go back to Redding's rooms, supposing I had been there and killed. A murderer may return eventually to the scene of his crime, but not immediately. In a way it was the safest place for me, and in many ways it was not. If I got caught there it was all off with me. They'd convict me of killing Redding as surely as the sun shone. They would find all the necessary evidence planted on yours truly. Get me and burn me in a blaze of glory. As Billings put it, the risk "put mustard on that sandwich."

I found Billings easily enough, his bulldog sprawling at

his feet as he sat on a bench on the east side of the square, away from the fountain and the swarming Italian children. He was stolidly reading the sporting pages. Billings was heavy-set, but active enough on his feet. He was pink of his clean-shaved jowls and he looked like a sporting tavern-keeper, had this been England. He might be a racing man, a retired livery stable keeper; there was a suggestion of the horse about him that could not be denied. He found it valuable.

The bulldog gurgled deep in its throat at me; knowing a friend, while I sat down beside Billings and patted the big, affectionate brute. Billings's greeting was characteristic. There was no word of welcome.

"A dorg," he said pragmatically, "is a good pal, but 'e's hapt to give you aw'y. I 'ad a friend who was took, becos of his dorg. It was a scenthound, a setter. The dicks got 'old of it while 'e was in quod. They get a tip where 'e might go an' they tyke the dorg there, an' 'e finds 'im, proud as Punch to do it. 'E 'ad a swell disguise, too, better'n yourn."

All this in tones that could not be heard five feet away. I laughed. It was his way of giving advice.

"I had to put off getting properly fixed up," I told him. "Wait till you see me then."

He looked at me with kindly eyes, as one might look at a younger brother, somewhat. There was real affection in them.

"Don't you forget that," he said. "Dorgs an' wimmen. Give you aw'y dead to rights, because they love yer, an' you them." He had been many years in the States. He used the argot of both sides of the pond, but he could not handle his h's. That was something that would help to identify him, but he had never yet been hauled in. Not once.

"How about yourself?" I asked.

"I've 'ad my weaknesses. This 'ere's the third dorg of 'is breed for me. But I married an' my missis, while she lived, was too downy to ever give me aw'y. She could myke the police commissioner look like a kid in the infant clarss, she could. Besides, I've quit, I've 'ad good luck and I'm quittin' while the quittin' is good."

My mouth parched suddenly.

"Quit?" I said.

"Dead. I've finished that lock, Kid. I got it so I can't pick it myself, so you can know it's good. I've got it patented and it's as good as sold. Cash and royalties. I'm tykin' out second citizenship papers and I'm settlin' down. Respectable and respected. Now, what can I do for you?"

He folded his paper, stuffed his pipe full of the shag he got imported some way, lighted the vile stuff and set his eyes on my face. I told him the whole story, leaving Kate out of it, from the time I reached New York. It was obvious that I had broken prison.

He heard me through, stolidly. I felt it was no use. I would have to go alone and do the best I could. Then I saw his eyes light up. I had not belittled the risks. The situation appealed to his sportsmanship. I think he knew already he was going to be bored with respectability.

"Quittin' on your own 'ook, and obliging a friend, is two different matters, Kid," he said as he laid his big but wonderfully well-shaped hand on my knee. "Your foster dad was twenty-four carat fine, 'e was. You ain't what I'd call pinchbeck yourself. I've never took a job that 'ad this

Redding mixed up in it. I don't know 'is mob. They're gettin' mighty slick and tony, these days, all of 'em. Fences calling themselves commission men! I like a straight job on a can. We'll myke it 'arf past one, Kid. Meet me at the Grand Central. I'll come out of the subw'y. We'll put the job across for the syke of your old man. 'E was all of that to you and a good pal to me. 'E'd like to know I've perfected the lock. Always advised me to do that. I'll bring what's needed. Now, you stroll off. If Redding 'ad anything tucked out of sight, we'll get it. If there's any one else there before us or coming after us, we'll get it just the syme."

THAT WAS BILLINGS. He might be a peterman—or have been—but he was regular. At one thirty he came up out of the subway. I expected to see him have some sort of a bag, perhaps camouflaged to look like a briefcase or a doctor's satchel, but he apparently had nothing more formidable than a cane. Everything, from chilled steel wedges to levers that fitted up like a fishing rod, was stowed away in heavy chamois leather casings. He was equipped like a dressing case, but nothing chinked, the topcoat did not seem bulky. If he had stepped on the scales he would probably have run the hands up round three hundred, but he walked easily, a substantial citizen out a bit late, with a friend.

I gave him a general idea of the layout and he grunted as he took it all in.

"Might try the window you went out of, or the roof," he said. "It depends on the w'y the land lies when we get there." I didn't get his meaning properly until we were on the corner of the block, passing a man obviously mailing a letter.

"That's a lookout," he said softly. "Works for 'Soup' Riley.

He don't know me. He just came in from Chi. Soup's helper
got stuck on a jane in a show and left town. This cove—
Evans—had a tip-off to Soup and he took him on. My
business to know all these things. Looks to me, Kid, as if
Riley was on our job. Not much to crack in this block. Soup
may work for Redding's racket, or what was Redding's. Do
you think that nigger'll know you?"

"Not with these clothes and this wig," I answered.

"You never can tell for sure about niggers," said Billings,
"but I guess we'll take the chance. We can't go climbing fire
escapes. Riley may have two men outside. I'll handle it."

We walked confidently in as the colored boy opened the
door. He had not much chance to observe me. I took my
hat off immediately to show my blond hair, but Billings
flashed a star on the lad, who batted his eyes.

"We're from headquarters," said Billings, with just the
correct rough inflection. "Now where's this apartment of
Redding's? Bring along your pass key and myke it snappy."

He was gruff and official. There had been police there,
off and on, all day. The operator was too impressed to
notice the British accent. The boldness of the move carried
through. The boy let us off, turned the key. I stood with my
hand on the door turn, ready to open it.

"You're tellin' no one we're here, mind," said Billings
impressively, taking the boy into apparent confidence. "If
any one comes you're not to interfere."

"Yessuh. No, suh." He vanished with the elevator, still
hypnotized by the star. It was a real one. Billings believed
in details.

We slipped inside the door and stood still, listening,
tense. The inner door was closed. I set my ear to the panels

and nodded at Billings who had switched on a hooded flash-torch. I had heard a sound. Then I gave way to the expert. He moved the handle imperceptibly, noiselessly, and I switched off, got my gun ready.

If Soup Riley was inside he might have saved us time, but there might be trouble ahead. There was a faint light inside the room and I saw Billings's bulk drift in. I followed.

There was a portable lamp on the door with a funnel-shaped shade. It had been brought by Soup, socketed in to a floor plug. It showed where a section of the paneling had been moved aside. An open safe showed, the inner door wide, revealing shelves with papers and books on them.

A man squatted on his heels, examining something. Billings motioned with his hand for me to stay where I was. Then, softly as a big cat, his pliable cane poised by the smaller end, he swung it as the man gave a little grunt of satisfaction and started to rise. The top of the cane, which had no handle, struck the man where skull and neck join and he pitched forward, seeming to try and stand on his head before he collapsed.

"Easy as pickin' rarsberries," said Billings, kneeling beside him, looking' up at me with a grin. " 'Ere's what 'e was after. Us, too, I bet."

IT WAS A combination wallet and memorandum book, well worn, with the initials J.R. in gold on the outside. I glanced quickly at the contents of the notebook, riffling the leaves. Names, figures! Notes that would have to be deciphered. No addresses that I could see, but I was well satisfied. Here was the matter Redding had relied upon to prove certain things in certain contingencies, hoping, perhaps, the fool, to hold it over the heads of the men who had got rid of him.

"Better slope," whispered Billings. "Leave the layout as it is. 'E never knew what 'it 'im, or who. Don't want his lookout to get wonderin' why 'e's been so long. Come on."

Just then the phone rang. It had been muffled cleverly and the sound was subdued so that it would not have carried through a closed door, yet it stopped us in our tracks, alarmed by that sibilant sound.

Something impelled me to answer it, despite Billings's mute protest. It was a French type of instrument and as I lifted the horizontal one-piece mouth and ear combination the bells buzzed again.

"Hello?" I called in a whisper.

"Who's this?"

"Soup. Who's this?"

"Gus Schumann. Have you got it?"

"Sure."

"*Gut!*" There was relief in the guttural syllable. "You are to bring it right away to my blace. The chief will be waiting."

I hung up. Gus Schumann was right. The chief would be waiting for a long time. There had been the name Schumann in the notes. Also just "Shu," and "G.S."

"Let's go," I said. The wallet was in my pocket. We left the lamp burning beside the senseless Soup Riley. He would come out of it in a few minutes and make his get-away. He had come in through the fire escape. The screen was removed. I did not touch the rest of the safe's contents. I knew I had what I wanted.

We rang the elevator bell and descended.

"All right, son," said Billings. "We'll handle this from the outside if anything breaks. Remember, you're dumb."

"Dumb, deef an' blind, suh. Done seen too much, heerd too much, an' talked too much, all day."

"He'll know you," I said to Billings as we went into the street after a careful survey for the lookout.

"He saw nothin' but the badge. If he did, they've got to pick me up first. I'm leavin' for Washington to-morrow, Kid, to see after my patent. They've never given me the third degree yet. I'm a respectable locksmith, an inventor who's protectin' cans, not openin' them. Riley opened this one. He didn't have to use soup on it, either. Them wall safes are always jokes."

He handed me his cane as we turned the corner. He nudged me to watch the figure of the lookout, Evans, who was lighting a cigarette, glancing over the excavation at the building we had left. The stick was heavy and flexible. It was formed of rings of leather compressed over a steel rod. They make them in penitentiaries. I gave it back to him and said "Good night," hailing a cab as Billings went on down the street, looking like a man who had just come from a poker club, or was on his way to one. A good deal of the sportsman about Billings.

The names in the notebook, as yet did not mean much. But they would. Clews would tie them up; and there was a card in a fold of the wallet, among others, that gave the name of August Schumann, Gem Broker, with his office address, down town. That was a live lead. I was going to cultivate the acquaintance of Gus Schumann, later on. It was wise to let things blow over.

Before I turned in I had the contents of that wallet and notebook by heart.

4

A DARING RAID

I WAS ON Long Island. Paul Standing. No more of Richard Pemberton. Blessing had achieved a masterpiece. There were no visible scars. He had changed the shape of my nose, working on the bone from inside. He had drawn my skin back beyond my ears, loosened it at the scalp, changed subtly the contour of my whole face. The slant of the eyes was different, the eyebrows changed, and the shape of the mouth.

On the whole, the effect was not displeasing. Two weeks had passed. I had dressed my own stitches and now they could not be seen, though my growing hair would have covered them. In a few days I could discard the wig and my own hair, dressed to match, would replace it.

As Paul Standing I went out a little in my friend's launch, walked more, played some golf, made a few acquaintances, and was understood to be writing a novel. The search for Convict 6439 was still going on. They had done some expensive tearing down at Ossining without finding hiding place or prisoner, but the warden still hoped. The papers had forgotten me, forgotten the murder of Redding. It had served its sensation. Another transatlantic plane had been lost, election day was closing in.

I was safe. There had been no mention of a burglary in the dead man's apartment. Soup Riley had got clear, though I imagined he must have had a bad quarter of an hour with the chief. Who that was I could not determine. There were five names in the little book, only one address. But I did not despair. There had once been six in the mob. There were only five now. Redding was out. One!

There is a touch of the melodramatic in all of us. I wished that I could have sent a telegram to all the others with just that single word "One." Later I might carry out that plan. It appealed to me, as it did to Monte Cristo. Like him I had escaped from prison, bent on revenge. I fed on it. Like Monte Cristo I was rich, having recovered my securities from safety deposit in Philadelphia. I was established. I practiced my new gait and mannerisms.

I was beyond the law. The mob might get me, but that was another deal.

Even if they bested me, with their odds of five to one, their resources, and their brains, nobody would ever be able to say that my dead body was that of Richard Pemberton.

Winter was occasionally in the air, but it was still mild. The trees were bare. There was a certain melancholy apparent. The country clubs had only desultory visitors. Some of the big houses still entertained over the weekend, but people were preparing to go south. And I was lonely. I read, at times, and went over my plans and hugged my revenge.

My nearest neighbor had what is called a show place. He was a financier named Penton, a power on the Street and in national affairs. I had met him casually at the club to which, through my friend, I was given privilege.

Thanksgiving was drawing near. The word and the day

had little enough in common with me, yet there was a feeling of festivity abroad, a gathering of clans, that emphasized my state. Families were gathering, making their preparations for the meetings here and there. Naturally, if I was ever mentioned, I was supposed to have my own connections. I would have given out that impression had I received any invitations, but, beyond the law as I was, I was also outcast from society.

Kate Wetherill I would not dwell upon, banishing her from my thoughts. I had vanished, as she knew me, and I meant to stay out of her ken. But that Power that is outside ourselves, ruling with a mysterious force—Fate, if you will—governed otherwise.

I WAS STRIDING along, swishing at dead plants that had fulfilled their mission, casting their seeds, wishing I had a dog, but knowing I might make a friend there I must neglect; walking a narrow lane, alone; when the swift roadster passed me. I stepped aside, for the road was muddy and a car had to keep in the tracks or skid. There was one person in it.

I knew who it was before I saw her face. My heart pounded suddenly. I thought to light a cigarette and hide my head with my hands, but the patent lighter failed me and I reached for a match. The driver accelerated and passed me close. I narrowed my eyes, emphasizing their new slant, and raised my hat as I stood close to the ditch. Here was the test. It had been forced upon me. I flattered myself that my face was a mask and the car went by with Kate looking at me with a slight smile. The ordeal was over, but it left results. My retreat was ended. Tomorrow I would go back to New York, bury myself and then, emerging, take up my chase.

I heard the squeal of brakes as I stood lighting my cigarette with fingers that shook.

"Paul! Paul!—"

I was half tempted to break through the hedge, to run, to do any mad thing. But she had swung the car across the slippery lane, backed into a gap by a gate, turned and was coming back. I stood there, waiting. She had found me, known me. It was a thing set down, ordained.

"I was going to your place," she said. "Did you think I would not know you? I told you it took two to break a friendship. I am a guest of the Fentons, over Thanksgiving. They were talking of you. They are going to send you an invitation to Thanksgiving dinner."

"I cannot accept it," I said. "I am going away to-morrow."

"And I am driving you away, my friend? I was on the way to your place. I knew you had a telephone, but—"

She knew I would avoid her. It had been foolish of me to tell her my new name, yet I owed her that. I had no idea that she knew the Fentons, but the world is, as they say, not so large.

"You are not driving me away," I told her. "It is necessary for me to go"

"When did you plan to leave—really?"

I would not lie to her.

"After Thanksgiving."

Lonely as I was, it had seemed to me less solitary to spend the holiday on Long Island than in New York. There is no solitude like that of a great city.

"Then promise not to leave till then. I must see you again, Paul. You are not—in my mood. To-night. Then, if it must be, we can say *au ravoir.* You owe me something."

More than I dared tell her. But in the end I promised witless things. To stay, to accept the invitation I would receive and call at the Fentons after Thanksgiving dinner. I had no heart for a festive meal. And I cursed my weakness all the way back.

My friend had taken his own servant and I had got a man from an agency who did me well enough, cooked better than tolerably.

I was mulling over my Thanksgiving meal, still in plus fours, intending to dress later, when the telephone rang sharply, insistently, in the living room. Randall, my man, was outside in the kitchen and I heard him go to answer it, mumbling inaudibly close to the transmitter.

Like the phone in Redding's room, this one seemed to awaken vibrations in me. I called Randall.

"Who was that?" I asked sharply.

"A friend of mine, sir. They wanted to know if I could come over, later. If I could, sir?"

HE LIED. MY eyes held his and challenged the truth. I had already told him he could go out that evening and he had declined. His ferrety gaze blinked at me. I knew this message was for me, could only have come from one place.

"Where to?" I asked him. He hesitated, stammered a little.

"The—Rossiters, sir."

I had learned the day before at the club that the Rossiters had changed their plans at the last moment; they were away. There was trickery here. Just then the bell rang again, kept on ringing as I went to answer it.

"Paul! Thank God! Listen. Your man said you were out, on the way here, but I did not believe him. The Fentons have been robbed. They sent for six men from the Larken Agency to watch. The guests have a lot of jewels. Three of them were waiters. The rest—I recognized one of them when they came in. The man we saw at the After Dark— and later—that gunman. He recognized me, but I slipped away. I was close by the conservatory and I am upstairs now. I—"

The voice was shut off. The line was dead. Wires had been cut. I had no car. Fentons' was a mile away. If Fin Murray had recognized Kate, he would look for her again. I went back to the dining room.

"Excuse me, sir, but you can't go out to-night."

I wheeled and saw Randall, pale, outwardly respectful, but with a gun pointing at me.

"What do you mean?" I demanded. It looked as if I must be known, after all. But why had they left it to one man? Why delay it until now?

"Just this, sir. You can't go out. If you try I shall have to stop you."

I forced a laugh, sat down in my place.

"You seem quite insistent about it," I said. "Well, if I can't go out, I can at least finish my dinner." I picked up my half-finished glass. I am not much of a drinker, but I had indulged on this occasion. The tumbler was half full of Scotch, easy enough to get, charged with White Rock.

"You can get on with that presently, sir," said Randall. I could see that he was nervous, but his hand was steady enough, though there was sweat on his forehead. "You carry a gun, sir. In your hip pocket. I'll have to take it over. Put your hands up."

"You've got a precious gall, Randall," I said. "But you've got a gun. I suppose you want me to stand?"

"If you please, sir." I damned his trained politeness as I stood up. He started to move around back of me and I let him have whisky, White Rock, glass and all full in his face. It blinded him for a second, as the thin glass cut his flesh, drawing blood, and I upset the table on him and leaped. I had him down. He fought like a cornered lynx with a desperate strength I never expected to find in him. I suppose he thought I was going to kill him.

We struggled for the gun and it was discharged, the powder blast slightly scorching my cheek as I ground his right wrist with my left hand and twisted my right free, driving for his jaw.

He collapsed. He was far from an athlete, and as he lay there panting, I took the gun away from him as easily as one may take a toy from a rebellious child.

"Now," I said fiercely, coldly, "just where do you come in on all this, Randall? I want it straight, and all of it. If I think you're lying you'll never talk again."

I SET THE muzzle of his own gun against his temple. His eyes rolled up, held abject terror. It was not just the fear of death. He was looking at something he had not before noticed. I found out eventually that it was my wig, slid awry in the struggle. If I had known that then I might have killed him.

What saved Randall, I suppose, was my relief in finding out that he knew less than I surmised.

"For God's sake, Mr, Standing, sir, don't shoot! I was forced into it. I couldn't help myself. I'll tell you—"

It was an ordinary enough story he stammered out, plausible, too. The Fentons were not the first family to have their house ransacked, their guests' jewels stolen on Long Island. Spies had been planted among the servants before this last coup of getting rid of the agency detectives and replacing them with their own men.

One of these house spies had met Randall in the village. He had known him as a more or less amateur crook, having met at a fence's.

It had been known that I had accepted the Fentons' bid, but was coming after dinner. It did not suit their plans to add to chances. Randall had been detailed to hold me at my place, promised a small share.

Five minutes later I had bound him to his own bed, put out my lights, and locked the house. I ran along the muddy road to "Gulls' Haven," as Fenton called his place, praying I would not be too late.

I ran steadily, not to be out of wind in an emergency. But I knew how quickly such rackets were pulled off when they were well conceived, and it was fifteen minutes after the telephone had been cut before I reached the side entrance to the elaborate gardens at Gulls' Haven.

I had already heard the noise of powerful motors in full rhythm, starting off, in full speed, mufflers open, then closed, the sound diminishing. As one neared the house, blazing with light, the grounds were terraced. Gulls' Haven stood on an elevation, almost a hill for Long Island.

I raced up low, broad steps, ran along the front of the house toward the main entrance and saw a plane, an amphibian, lift up from the water of the Fentons' anchorage, rising like a startled duck, scuttering over the surface, zooming up, climbing, roaring away over Long Island Sound, north to Connecticut; north and a little west, by the Big Dipper. I saw the flames spurt from the exhaust pipes. They had made their get-away, by plane and motor. And they had divided. Those two departures came too pat to be anything else.

The front doors opened before I rang. Several men guests came out on the top terrace, excited, self-important, inefficient. Then Fenton saw me.

"Standing!" he said. "You know what's happened? We've been robbed! Thieves among my own servants, in league with these fake detectives. They've cleaned us out. My wife's diamond necklace! Mrs. Vanstetter's pearls! They must have got a quarter of a million dollars' worth!"

I could see him staring at me, wondering why I was not dressed. And I had a gun in my hand. They were all alike in a physical emergency, these kings of finance and scions of society. Barking up wrong trees and always off the scent. The damned fools were beginning to wonder whether I hadn't something to do with the racket.

"TO THE DEVIL with you and your jewels!" I said to Fenton. "Where is Miss Wetherill?"

He repeated it like a parrot.

"Where is Miss Wetherill?"

"She telephoned for me when they started to rob you. Slipped up through the conservatory. The wires were cut."

Fenton, they say, is noted for lightning decisions, swift swoops and juggernaut judgments on the Street. Now he gaped at me. A haggard butler, not quite demoralized despite treachery among his staff, caught my eye.

"Where would she phone from, going through the conservatory? Show me," I rapped out at him. Mrs. Fenton had her wits about her.

"I haven't seen Kate since this happened," she said. "Show Mr. Standing, Rogers."

I followed him into the conservatory, lit with fairy lamps among the palms, the moon streaming through the half dome of glass.

The long French windows were wide open. A balcony outside with scrolled iron work. Caught in one of the hammered curves was a strip of chiffon, sewn with silver spangles. Other spangles glittered on the floor as Rogers switched on the lights.

"It looks like they'd taken her, sir," he said. "That was the material she was wearing."

5

A COLD TRAIL

THE LOCAL POLICE came and, later on, others who considered themselves experts. Reporters arrived, avid for news, descriptions of the jewels, pictures for special editions of the tabloids. They collected evidence and personal experiences, they found some evidence that had been overlooked and sagely called it clews.

"We've got an idea who pulled this," one of the cracks said to Fenton. "We'll have a line on them before the day's out. An inside job, in a way. Those who were planted here made their getaway with the others, but we may be able to get something out of the servants."

It was the old formula, the old expression of confidence from the dicks. The reporters grinned and winked at each other when they heard it. Insurance representatives scoffed less openly. One of the newspaper men winked at me. At any other time I might have winked back.

Here they were, the hounds of the law, seeking a new scent. Here I was, a man who had baffled all of them, a man whom they were still seeking, a reward offered for me, accused of one murder and suspected to know something of another, not to mention having broken prison—right in their midst, talking to them, giving them information, being questioned, about to be featured in a paragraph or two of the story that had broken so opportunely after a dull Thanksgiving. And they did not know me, accepted me at face value as Paul Standing, friend of the host and at least one of the guests, himself invited, arriving at the moment of the big thrill, the abduction of Kate Wetherill.

That was the big story to the newspaper boys and the police—the human element. I am not so sure it was to some of the dowagers who had lost their gems—all heirlooms, to hear them tell it—that mere insurance could never replace.

If they had known who I was, they would have pinned this robbery on me beyond question, and once more shown how infallible they were. These were hard times for the force. They had been shaken up until they frothed by an irate commissioner, and still racketeers carried on their gang wars with impunity, shot each other down with baby machine guns and carried tear bombs. They came in from Chi to New York and vice versa. They held up armored cars and pay rolls until the public was getting stirred up.

To have caught Richard Pemberton masquerading at Gulls' Haven, charge him with escape from the penitentiary and the killing of John Redding, bondbroker, and claim he was undoubtedly the leader of the Fenton robbery—they would all have won feathers for their caps indeed.

The evidence came down to this. Three waiters had been hired by the Fentons' butler from a supposedly reputable agency. They had been there about two weeks. It was hard to get servants for the country at this time of the year. They seemed to be all right. Probably they had used the names of decent people, given their references as their own. It was done often enough.

The six detectives hired from the Larken Agency to guard the property of the guests had been met at the station by a car and a liveried driver. He had, he said, been sent for them. As a matter of fact no car had been sent. The butler, who had arranged for them, considered they should be able to arrive under their own power.

The real detectives were driven along a side road leading to the servants' and delivery entrance, hidden from the house by shrubbery. They did not get much further. They were promptly stuck up as they got out of the car, ignominiously bound with insulated wire, gagged, left in a toolhouse where the searching police discovered them after the coup.

There were tracks under the balcony where the spangled chiffon strip had hung. The trail of a man landing heavily. The dicks looked wise and took measurements. It was obvious, since there was only one set of footprints, a man's, that the girl had been borne by him. If she had screamed, no one heard her. She might have been knocked senseless. But they had those footprints.

As if a smart thief with a cut-in on a quarter of a million—it might simmer down to a quarter of that by the time it was fenced, but it was a good haul—would not change his shoes at the earliest moment and destroy the ones he had worn! That the raiders were wise hands was shown by the fact that the man who brought in a dispatch case from the library to hold the loot wore gloves. They all wore gloves, as servants, for that matter. They left no fingerprints about on dishes or woodwork. It was a clean job.

The bullet, aimed at Schumann's gargoyle-face, spanged against the steel

There were a few spangles beside the footprints, a few more that went with the tracks to the hard road, too hard to hold tire marks.

One or two people had seen the amphibian light in the anchorage, but thought nothing of it. It was presumed to be bringing up-to-date guests. Several had come in launches that were really small yachts. As for the powerful car I had heard, while it was probably the getaway machine, it would not attract special notice. It looked as if the girl had been taken in the motor.

THE MEN SENT after Randall, my enterprising servant, found him gone. They thought he had managed to untie his bonds. I knew differently; but I was not arguing or posing as any kind of an expert. I believe that he yelled and told some cock-and-bull story to a passer-by who released him and then later, hearing the news, was afraid to come forward. The pantry window never closed properly and it was open. I felt it best to mention Randall, to help my own position.

It looked like another Long Island mystery, with the added zest of Kate Wetherill's disappearance. It meant publication of her picture, a vivid story of her personality. Another sensation to feed the subway travelers, looking for vicarious romance and adventure, and for the blasé leisure class.

As for me, I formed my own theory. It might not be firmly based, but it had some sort of a foundation. I was not volunteering it; I would have been asked too many questions. Of necessity and choice I was going to play a lone hand, with indifferent cards dealt me. Not a pair or a sequence in it.

The names in Redding's notebook were: "R. Bower-man," sometimes "B." or "R.B." "Augustus Schumann," "Gus," "Shu," and "S."; "H.A. Mullett," generally set down as "Ham"; "H. Lee," "Lee," or "L"; and "Chief," which I took to be a title, remembering Schumann's instructions to the man he supposed was Soup Riley. There was one reference to "Cap" which was a little obscure.

I had made some deductions. There was an H.A. Mullett in the directory—dealer in woolen goods. Three R. Bower-mans—one of whom was a general broker of merchandise. Any amount of H. Lees. Schumann I knew as a gem broker. "Chief" was covered. Redding was gone.

It began to look to me like a ring, a mob run by the man called Chief, who would be what the police called the Master Mind. Stolen goods, from trucks, from warehouses, from cars en route or ferried across the river, could be handled beautifully and profitably. Lee undoubtedly handled a certain line. Fin had protected Redding, or tried to, when Redding was one of them. He would be one of other gunmen, other racketeers in the mob doing the actual work as laid out through the Chief.

This was the outfit that had killed Harvey Pemberton, my benefactor, because he knew too much about them and would not join them. Murdered and robbed him, framed me. One had been disposed of, though not by my hand. I was going to get the rest.

This Fenton robbery looked like Schumann's job to me. He would dispose of the jewels easily enough to his trade as unset gems, and he would, in the course of time, get something close to their real value. The jewels would be taken to him, as other goods would be taken to Bowerman, Mullett and Lee. There were no middlemen. These were supreme fences under almost perfect cover.

Kate had said that Fin recognized her and she him, probably simultaneously. He would remember where he had seen her, at the "After Dark," with me. When they were on duty, men of his calling missed little. He had seen me again, in Redding's rooms. Kate had worn the mask of lace and her cloak, which Fin had not seen at the night club, but would he not jump to the almost obvious conclusion that she was the "scrappin' moll" that had bested him? I thought so. In that case what would they do to her? It was maddening to contemplate, but necessary.

FIN WOULD NOT know me again. The man I was then was gone, merged unrecognizably in Paul Standing. But they would try to make her tell who it was had been with her, try to break her down. Especially if Redding's death was still a mystery to them. They knew that I was out of Sing

Sing. They could understand well enough that I would be disguised, but they would not be likely to think that disguise permanent. It would do them no good if they did—unless they knew how I looked now.

But my ends were subservient to the rescue of Kate. That and the discovery of who had taken the jewels might break together, if I was successful; but I could not appear against them without disclosing my methods, how and where I had picked up the trail. That did not matter now. Her release was paramount.

I doubted if Schumann was along. It was absurd to think that he would risk himself in the open. But the gems would be taken to him. How? In the plane or the car? And which was Kate in? Her ultimate fate would rest with the mysterious Chief, I believed. Fin would give some reason for carrying her off, but I believed, I prayed earnestly, that he would not talk overmuch immediately. For an organization to be successful, as Redding's notes indicated it was, there must be a head, a ruler, who would be sure to resent any usurpation of his supreme authority.

That she was in dire peril was certain. Hours had passed and no clew turned up better than the one I clung to: Schumann. It was the only lead.

I took an early train to New York with money in my pocket, the best of all weapons. I ate, solely because there was time and because a man is a fool to let his fuel run low if he can prevent it. At nine o'clock I was at the building where Schumann carried on his business. He had a suite of three offices, according to the directory on the ground floor.

There was no one there. I had been afraid of that. I had never expected to find Schumann, but only to discover, by some trick, where he lived. I came back to the elevator starter. I had not changed my clothes, but plus-fours walk the city with hatless heads nowadays from Wall to the end of Fifth Avenue. To him I was sufficiently normal, my clothes a little sporty but expensive.

"You don't know where I could find Schumann, or one of his men, do you?" I asked. "It's important."

I have often noticed on the trail, whether a puncher chasing cattle thieves or a town dick after crooks, that the "sign" is hardest to find where you expect it to be easy, and the other way around. The breaks are uneven for pursuer and pursued. The starter gave me mine, nonchalantly.

"You won't find any of 'em in town. Off over the week-end for the holidays. Pretty lucky. We're runnin' empty cars. Old Schumann has beaten it to the country. They say he's got a swell dump up near Carmel. I'll bet he's stagin' a party. That boy steps out."

I knew Carmel. I had stopped at the Lakeside Inn and caught bass in the lake and the surrounding reservoirs, where one may fish and boat without motors, but where it costs fifty dollars to be found swimming. If Schumann lived there, I should find him without much trouble. The question was, how to go?

The way of a plane, like that of "the eagle in the air," is hard to know, especially when it flies after nightfall and lands before daylight. But Carmel was almost due north-by-west from Gulls' Haven. I doubted if it was more than fifty miles air-line over Long Island Sound and across Connecticut to the little county-seat of Putnam County, New York. Twenty minutes for a fast ship, thirty at the most.

And, though motors were forbidden, it might alight unobserved after dark in one of the many reservoirs in the neighborhood. An emergency might be imagined, or pleaded, if any one interfered, which was a remote possibility. The reservoirs were only irregularly patrolled, seldom, if ever, at night. But that was where that plane had gone. It did not need the confirmation of a hunch to decide that.

Probably the loot had gone with it in the dispatch case. Kate, too? It seemed not, on the inconclusive evidence, but Schumann was there. It was quite likely that the car had gone there as well.

TO GET A plane in New York one must go to Long Island. To be seen landing might expose me to the watchfulness of Schumann, accidentally or otherwise. The country is hilly, with few landing places, none that would not advertise my arrival.

Schumann would imagine himself safe. I did not flatter myself unduly that the ring was as yet frightened very much over any revenge I might attempt, even if they thought it was I who had been in Redding's rooms the night he was killed. Later, they might, but they were strongly protected. They had boldness, though one or two, like Redding, might be weak in spots. But it would probably not be too easy to get entrance to Schumann's country home. I might even have to wait until dark. Still, I was not going to waste any time getting there.

I had no car of my own. There is more red tape wrapped around the hiring of a "Drive It Yourself" machine than most people imagine. I preferred a motorcycle. They can make time, they are not so easily traced, and they can be hidden where a car cannot. I bought overalls, cap and goggles and purchased a four-cylinder racer for spot cash. It had a side car. I hoped for a return passenger, though I had little idea then whom I would carry in that bathtub-looking contrivance, and how.

I was over the Harlem River by noon, trundling along like a chap out to take his girl friend for a ride. I tucked my wig away. My hair was long enough now without it, and I did not mean to take off the cap. I broke no laws save the Sullivan Law, forbidding me the gun in my side pocket. There was not a great deal of traffic. The day was raw, the year too far on for picnicking. It rained a little at White Plains, but stopped after it made the roads slippery. They were good, but not all cement, and I made fine time, considering, once I got beyond traffic.

It was half after two when I swung round the sharp curve by the bank at Brewster, turned left over the railroad bridge and up the hill. Carmel was only a few minutes away. There were a few guests at the Lakeside Inn where I spoke to the owner, who utterly failed to recognize me. I had begun to be and feel a different man inside. There was no trace left of Richard Pemberton now.

Schumann had a place on a ridge between two reservoirs Mahopac way, a stone building with a tower, back from the road. He liked fishing, it seemed, and he liked privacy, though he often had guests. I did not have to ask for this. Listening is, nine times out of ten, the surest way and often the quickest of getting information. There were localites in the comfortable main room of the tavern who soon showed what they knew.

I was torn between anxiety and discretion. It would be dark in two hours. Lake Carmel was the color of dull steel, matching the sky, both whipped with gusts of wind that stirred the fallen leaves and bowed the pines. There is a route to New York by way of Lake Mahopac that would take me past Schumann's place and I asked a direct question or two that let it be assumed I was on my way back to the city. I got a meal served to me and smoked a reflective but troubled cigar before I had my tank filled and strode my motorcycle once more. The side car was provided with a hood, a waterproof apron.

It looked like dirty weather before many hours. The sun was hidden. There was an elderly man on the lake who was rowing slowly to shore at the inn. I knew him well enough, a persistent fisherman who visited the lake every season. He looked up and gave me a wave of his hand that startled me for a moment, though it meant nothing but an expression of his genial nature. He probably took me for a chap off on a holiday trip which was being spoiled by the murky day.

I skirted the curve of the lake, crossed the railroad, passed some summer homes and bungalows and soon came to a stretch, lonely on a day like this, that lay between Carmel and Mahopac. To left and right there showed sheets of gusty water, bending pines and hemlock, a dreary setting.

I halted, kicked down the rest and stopped my pulsing motor. The machine had run splendidly and I had not pressed it on account of its being new. I dismounted and fiddled with the motor, looking up and down the road. On the right were the iron gates that guarded the twisting way leading to Schumann's. I could not see it now, but I had glimpsed the top of the stone tower farther back. It stood dark and solid and Teutonic.

6

SCHUMANN'S CASTLE

THE GATES WERE locked as I tried them, after assuring myself there was no one in sight. The place was posted. A wall of native field stone ran round the estate that could be climbed. Again I looked and listened, then ran the cycle up a bank and hid it among the high weeds close to the wall. I made the top and lay on it, spying out the terrain. The house was some distance back. Schumann had chosen well for privacy. The district was not yet built up.

His place was on the watershed. The owner had reserved privileges when he sold out to the water company. Schumann himself, perhaps. But no others would be able to purchase similar sites. He would never have near neighbors.

I went on foot up a slope. Schumann's big house was in plain sight, lights in the lower part of it. I could see other buildings, a garage, I imagined, and a spring house, another for his engines. Carmel was on a power line, but the gossips said that Schumann had his own lights. That might be worth while.

I scrambled up that hill through stumpy sumach and leafless briers, and finally found a sort of trodden trail that led where I wanted. The darkness was sifting down, the

wind increasing, momentarily. There was evergreen shrubbery near the house, a hedge of hemlock between it and
the other buildings.

It seemed to me that there were preparations going on
for dinner in the kitchen, a gathering in a room on the
ground floor beneath the tower. The windows were fairly
high, and screened, and the sills were narrow. Outside the
kitchen I heard a jabber of Chinese. I would not have been
surprised at Japanese, but I knew the difference in the sing-
song dialect. Chinese servants are good and discreet, but in
New York they are hard to get, preferring independence.

I examined all the entrances. Locked. It was at once
a disappointment and a reassurance. Those within were
taking precautions. I had found them in conference. Kate
might be in one of the dark rooms of the tower. Somehow
I did not think so, feel so. I believed that if she had been
near, I would have known it.

I crouched by the hemlock hedge. It was early yet. I had
my quarry corralled. Some one might come out soon. I
saw a big car parked on the road, not taken into the garage,
and it cheered me. I had come in time to see some of the
play, at least.

Now, as the wind gathered strength and went sough-
ing through the trees, whispering through the hedge, the
shrubbery, I was glad of my overalls, glad I had eaten at
the inn. It was getting bitterly cold. Darkness came ahead
of normal, without stars, black and dismal, moaning, the
air chilled from the water, a damp atmosphere that struck
to the bone.

An oblong of light showed as a man came out, going to
the little powerhouse. He had left the door ajar and I went

swiftly toward it, quiet and quick as a shadow shrouded in darkness. I opened it and slipped in.

It was an entry way, lit with an electric bulb, doors to left and right and ahead. To the right was the babble of Oriental tongues, the clatter of pots and dishes. I went ahead, through a swinging door into a pantry which was dark, using my hooded flash light.

Then came a dining room with two shaded wall lights gleaming so that I switched off my torch. Schumann did himself well. The place was paneled in walnut, there was a thick carpet on the floor, trophies of stuffed heads on the wall, a carved buffet, carved chairs, a centerpiece of evergreens and a few late autumn leaves.

Next a long salon, tapestried. A built-in organ occupied one end, the windows were heavily curtained, recessed. Heavy, Germanic furniture, many pictures, a radio cabinet, valuable rugs.

I HEARD MORE voices, one of them high-pitched, excited, angry. The merest thread of light came from beyond folding doors. The big room I was in, with the dining room, covered the floor of the main building, I calculated. That strip of yellow came from the tower.

A bell rang and I dodged back of the curtains. A Chinaman came shuffling on felt slippers, dressed in dark, native costume. He advanced to the folding doors, which he parted.

"What you like?" he asked.

There followed laughter, the petulant voice was drowned out. A volley of orders for cocktails, liquors. A thick voice ordering kümmel. That was Schumann's, louder and freer than I had heard it over the phone at Redding's, but unmistakable.

"All light, I get," said the Chinese servant. "You say once mo', please. I like get light."

They repeated, laughing, and the man came back, muttering to himself.

I sat there on the wide window ledge, the cold metal of my gun warming in my hand, straining on the leash, but unlike a hound, holding myself in. I waited till the man came back, bearing a heavy tray. I let him pass through, serve, and return, vanishing. Then I went forward on the balls of my feet, got the fingertips of my left hand between the doors, slid one back, and surveyed the scene.

It was a notable one. They did not notice the open doors, nor me. I saw the host at the center of a long table, raising his glass. I saw about him a gang of racketeers, excited, well-dressed for the most part, though some wore sweaters. And I counted them. Eight in all, responding to a toast.

The room was a library, according to the bookshelves. They were all at one end, about the big table. And that shot rainbows. Not my kind of rainbows, but scintillating flashes from a heap of jewelry. Loot from Gulls' Haven!

I was halfway to them before they saw me. Glasses suspended between the oak and their throats as they stared at the man in a singleton of denim, capped and goggled, a gun in his hand that swung in a leisurely arc that included all of them.

One man, on his feet, gasped like a goldfish.

"Stand up, all of you!" I said. "With your hands above your eyebrows!"

They obeyed like sheep. Without question they were

armed; but they obeyed. I saw Fin—saw his hand creeping down toward his shoulder. To him I was an enigma in cap and goggles and singleton who might be outwitted.

"Up with them, you on the right, you, *Fin!*" I snapped.

He stiffened, as much to the name, as the command. I was puzzling them, as I meant to.

"Just to show you I can shoot," I said, "I'm taking Shu's glass. I won't hurt him if he keeps still." There was no mistaking which was Schumann, aside from his position at table. He was the one who had gasped at my entrance, not especially from fear, perhaps, though his heavy-jowled face grew mottled as my gun barked and the bullet smashed the crystal and flung glass and kümmel in a frosty spray. They did not know what to make of me at all, which suited me, though Schumann's eyes were calculating now.

He was beginning to piece things together, I think; the loss of Redding's notebook plus what Fin might have told him. And he was not without his resources, as I was soon to learn.

"What do you want?" he asked in his throaty voice.

I LAUGHED. I had begun to cultivate a certain quality of voice to fit Paul Standing, but I did not use it now. I talked coarsely in tone and phrase.

"You got it right in front of you," I said. "The stuff from Gulls' Haven. You guys think you're dead wise, but this time you got tipped off, see? Thanks for doin' the work. And don't get gay when I back off with it. I'm doin' the collectin', but I didn't come here alone. So you play safe."

I had staggered them, sown doubt and dissension among them. Do that to any mob and you've got them going. But it was not the racketeers I was after, but the principals, one

of whom was in front of me now. So far as I was concerned
I did not care how many Fentons they robbed of jewels;
how many warehouses they looted. I held no brief for the
law. But it was good business for me, just the same, to have
them glancing at each other and at Schumann while they
remained under the menace of my gun as its muzzle moved
in a steady arc.

Outside of Schumann, perhaps, there was not one of
them who did not pack a weapon and know how to use it.
It was not unlikely that every one of them had not merely
shot to kill, but had killed. I could not hope to get away
with all of them if trouble started even if I had bullets
enough to go round. They would get me about my third
shot and they knew it as well as I did. I saw Fin wet his lips
with the end of his tongue, knew he was very close indeed
to taking a chance despite my special warning.

It was a funny thing, but there was something about Fin
that I liked. I suppose it was because he had nerve. But I
kept paying particular attention to him.

Then Schumann spoke again.

"I don't know who you are or where you got your tip," he
said slowly, "but you seem to have the say of things right
now. You want the swag? Help yourself."

He said it pleasantly, almost jocularly, as if asking me
to help myself to ice and pass the bowl. "Ice" much of it
was, in thief-talk. There was the diamond necklace of Mrs.
Fenton and scores of other selected stones blazing away.
There were softly shimmering pearls in long strands, there
were rubies and emeralds blending their rays. Many of
them had been already taken from their settings and made
individual pools of light.

I pondered for a minute. Schumann was altogether too nice about it for plain resignation to hard luck. His eyes did not match his tone at all. They looked out at me from triangles of upper and lower lids and they were cruel, expectant, the eyes of a tiger.

I listened for the buzz of a distant signal, for any sound behind me. There was nothing audible or visible, but there was something in the air. They were all watching me with a furtive expectancy. I thought I could see the beginning of a derisive grin on some of their faces.

I advanced slowly, ill at ease, warned by my hunch to look out. I was a little uncertain of my next move, whether to take the jewels first, or their weapons, and I was wary of the Chinese in their quarters back of me. I could not watch the folding doors. There was no convenient Venetian mirror this time on the wall, only a tapestry of a boar-hunt back of Schumann, who was still standing, bending forward, ever so slightly.

A change, almost indefinable, came over his face. Fin's shoulders hitched slightly. My end of the room was set about with carved settees, a window on the left, on the right a fireplace where big logs were burning. Over the mantel were a trophy of medieval armor and two wooden shields painted with heraldic designs. On a small table was a dispatch case of leather. I had no doubt that this was the one that had come from Gulls' Haven. I wanted that, even more than I wanted the jewels, but all of them were nothing compared to news of Kate.

I took a step forward and I saw the edge of the big rug on which I was standing flip up, as if a sudden, stiff draft of wind had come through the floor and lifted it. Then with a whirring rush, so close that it fanned my face as it passed, there lifted a screen of steel, rising swiftly to the ceiling, toward one of the great beams of timber, cutting between me and them.

Another step, half a one and it would have got me, under the chin, tearing through my skull if it did not hoist me to crush it against the timber. It was a devilish device and a clever one. My bullet, aimed at Schumann, whose face looked like that of a triumphant gargoyle, spanged against the steel, so swift was the uprushing metal.

I RECOILED, MY smoking, useless gun in my hand. The clang with which the steel screen had socketed into a groove attached to the beam died away. It seemed to me I could hear a laugh, certainly the duller, hollow sound of wood shifting. They were gone, mocking me. I ran to the folding doors.

They were tight-locked, solid. The Chinese were in on the play or else the same connection that had released the screen had bolted the doors. Schumann had done that while he kidded me, who had thought myself so competent and masterly. Now I was trapped. The room had been fairly cut in half.

I could not budge the doors. I caught up a chair, but it smashed uselessly against the heavy oak. The window was locked, not merely by the catch.

I swung the broken chair against the glass. It was toughened, bullet-proof. I did not even mark it. They had me. But I was puzzled. I saw the headlights of first one and then another car as they rushed by the tower to the main road. Why did they leave me in Schumann's house while they fled with the loot? They might have been due in town to meet the chief. Schumann might feel he knew who I was—and the Chinese were still on hand.

I don't underestimate Chinks as fighters. They have many virtues, but they are cold-blooded and they are used to executions. The reservoir, two in fact, lay very handy for a weighted body and they would have no compunction about the purity of New York's water supply. It was not a pleasant moment and suddenly the lights went out.

I had my flash light, but the fire was better and I might need all that battery. A man's mind is either numb when he is in deadly peril or it works quickly. But the flickering light and shade was eerie and I could vision the Chinese coming on the other side of those doors. There might be trick panels here also.

I stood by the fire for a moment, then saw a long trident of iron, a devil-stick, for moving the big logs. I could smash the window, tough as it was, with that. Raising it like a javelin I saw the folding doors sliding softly apart. My yellow hatchetmen were coming.

I was prepared for them, whether they came with blade or gun, but hardly for the brutes that came in with a rush, their fangs plain in the firelight, their jaws slavering, their wild eyes gleaming like crimson spangles with the fire, growling deep in their throats as they turned and made for me.

Police dogs! That was the meaning of Schumann's sardonic laugh I had heard through the metal screen. Trained to watch the place against all strangers when the owner was away. They had probably been muzzled when I crept into the grounds, but now they were set on me. The doors had closed again, instantly, the moment they were let through. Three of them, ravening, half-wolves.

It was lucky I had picked up that devil-stick.

I drove it so hard, shifting my grip, that the blunt prongs went through the throat of the leading beast as it leaped straight for my throat. They held there for a moment as the weight of the brute sank it down and I tugged to free it. Another was at my chest, snarling and snapping. It tore away a section of my singleton suit. The loose, tough fabric saved me.

My weapon was free and its victim lay writhing on the floor, belching blood, gasping, done for. The third dog sprang and I swung on its skull. It cracked, split open, and the dog dropped beside the other. The stout iron was bent with the impact.

There was no time to raise it again before the second beast was on me again, undaunted, fierce, intent to kill. In a way they were magnificent brutes, but their courage was of the wolf, not the friend of man. I met the charge with my knee in its chest and bowled it over. It twisted like a flash, but I had dropped the iron and got my gun again. It took three bullets to stop the beast, and my leg covering was torn to strips with teeth and claws. But I was unscratched. It was all over.

I stood there panting with the fury of the swift battle. I pictured the Chinese outside the doors, listening. Presently they would come in. I was not waiting for that. I was very willing to get away from the place.

There was a cloth of soft brocade on the table beneath the dispatch case. The latter had Fenton's initials on it and his address—Gulls' Haven, Midshore, Long Island, inside the flap. Schumann made a mistake when he left that behind. Perhaps he had not noticed the lettering, but it was going to prove a petard for his hoisting, if I got it back to New York. I carefully wrapped the cloth about it. I had a plan for Schumann's undoing unless he was craftier than I gave him credit for.

I battered the toughened glass apart with the iron, more like wood pulp than transparent crystal. It made little noise as it tore rather than split. The wire beyond was simple. I heard again the distant sound of powerful cylinders. I caught a glimpse of headlights in a gap between the hills before they disappeared. They were taking the Carmel route. It made little difference.

7

AMBUSH

MY ONE DUTY was to get the best of those yellow men, search the house for Kate. There was, of course, the chance that they had taken her, that she had never been brought there at all; but I could not leave that risk open. Softly I dropped to the ground, gun in one hand, the dispatch case under my left arm.

A spurt of flame came out of a thicket as I lit, stumbling on a loose stone that saved me as a bullet went over my head and flattened on the stone wall back of me. I knelt and fired, twice, at the flash, matching a second shot that came wild while a figure pitched, rolling into the path and writhed there, clutching at the gravel. I ran forward, knowing I had got my man.

It was Fin. They had left their crack gunman behind, to make doubly sure of me. He was clawing at his "rod," trying to aim with hand and arm that refused to function. I kicked the weapon out of his hand and switched my light on him.

He was in bad shape, his face convulsed with pain, a crimson froth at his lips. I had got him through the right shoulder, smashing the bone, and through the lungs. Picking up his gun, I left him and went round the house swiftly and silently. There was a light in the little power house and

I looked in. There was a lighting plant, an automatic engine working, a pump chugging away somewhere. The garage doors were open, the place empty.

I tried the door I had entered before and it yielded. There was talk again on the right, low Chinese tones. And there was whispering beyond the door ahead of me. I opened the one on the left, using my flash. It was a little more than a closet with mops and brooms, a vacuum machine and, on a hook, a long coil of braided clothesline. I had struck gold.

The handles of the kitchen and entry doors were tied together. I took the rest of the coil and slowly entered the dining room. It was empty, but I vaguely saw two dim figures in consultation under the arch that led to the big living room. They were wondering what had happened beyond the folding doors to the ground-floor tower chamber, a little afraid. They must have heard the shooting and they were uncertain what to do.

Still more so in the second the ray fell on them, but they soon understood, with my gun as interpreter to emphasize my command. I bound them back to back, searched them and got a third gun and two nasty-looking knives that had never been designed for household purposes. I marched them crab-fashion to the closet, assured myself of the roping and locked them in.

There were two more in the kitchen, one the man who had taken in the drinks. Their stolid yellow faces broke up when they saw me, then settled again. That was not a cheery interview. I threatened one of them with a seat on the stove if he didn't say something beyond "no savvy" when I asked about Kate. I had them in cold blood and they were as afraid of death as men of any other country.

I was satisfied at last that she had never been there and I left them tied up and in the dark.

I locked every door on the outside before I went back to Fin. I did not figure on getting much out of him, if he was still alive. He was, and he managed a twisted grin. I felt sorry enough for him to see if there was anything I could do. Rain was beginning to fall again. He had tried his best to kill me this time, but once before he had held his hand—long enough for Kate to save the night. I owed him that. I could not leave him to die in the rain. There was the house, but he was bleeding badly, blue about the lips. He needed a doctor, quickly.

"You're a good shot, bo'," he said faintly. "You do in those dogs?"

"I've got the house cleaned up," I said. "I'm wondering what to do with you."

"You've got your rod an' mine, ain't you? There's just one thing I need, guy, and you can't give it to me. A sniff of snow. I'd go out smilin', then."

"If I knew where to get it for you, I would," I told him. He wanted it with all an addict's craving in extremity. If a man's got the habit, he has, that's all there is to that. **MY VOICE MUST** have carried conviction. He could not see me back of the ray.

"No kidding, guy? No kidding?" he asked pitifully.

"No kidding, Fin."

"There's nothin' I wouldn't do fer a shot."

They all talk like that, of course, when they need it. But I didn't think Fin was altogether a coke-fiend. He took it, like most of the racketeers, and now was when he most craved it.

"There's a place, bo', that ain't so far from here. Not more'n a couple of miles, off on a dirt road. There's a guy there that could fix me up. He's runnin' hooch now, stillin' some, but he'd take me in and he ain't a bad doctor at that."

He might be giving away a gang secret, or the man might be just a bootlegger. Fin was getting low, past caring much for anything but his coke. If the man handled drugs it was a risk to tell me, but, after all, whoever Fin might think I was, he had seen me after loot. Probably thought I was blackmailing Redding.

"I've got a side car, if you think you can stand it," I said to him. "I'll take you there, and when I get back to New York, I'll pass the word where you want so you can get a doctor."

"Gee, I'd stand ridin' on top of a dump wagon to get to Tony's. Listen, guy, you won't lose by this, see? You turn off on the first road to the left on the way to Mahopac. First left again. Secon' house on the right. Farmhouse. Dagoes. Ask fer Tony. Tell him it's Fin."

His voice trailed off. He had fainted from weakness. I bound up his wounds as best I could and then went down to get the motorcycle. They had left the gates unlocked in their haste, or the Chinese had been too excited to lock them. I lifted Fin into the side car I had hoped to use for Kate. My thoughts were of her. I did not feel much like a good Samaritan as I bundled him on the seat and drew the hood and windshield together. The rain was coming down in earnest now.

I had to get back to New York. Schumann was still my best lead. Fin was more selfish than grateful, I imagined. He was nothing now, unconscious, which was lucky for

him as we went along that villainous dirt road in a downpour that covered it with slithery muck, hiding the ruts
and holes. It nearly ditched us several times.

There was a light in the house he had spoken of. Two
hounds bayed dismally as I stopped and went round to the
back door, knowing the front would be locked, farmhouse
style, after dark. The family would be in the kitchen. They
were there all right. Seven stepladder children, two women,
one of whom was a muttering decrepit crone. The man was
a good picture of a Mafia bandit with his black shock of
hair, the red bandana at his throat, his glittering eyes and
ragged mustache.

"What you want?" he demanded fiercely. I wasn't looking
much myself with my torn singleton, dog blood and hair
smeared on it. "What you want?"

"Fin wants you. He's outside, hurt bad."

"Fin?" He rolled his eyes at me, spoke in rapid fire Italian with his wife.

"What's your name?"

"The Kid. If you don't hurry up Fin will be dead—*morto!*"

He came out at that with an old tarpaulin over his head
and shoulders. He kept his hand on his knife handle in his
belt until I opened the hood and flashed my torch.

"*Dio!* He ees *morto* now. I not touch."

It looked like it. The gunman's face was drained of blood.
My crude bandages were crimson with it, but his pulse was
beating. Tony opened an eyelid, felt over his heart, grum-
bling to himself in his own tongue. Then he reached in and
picked Fin up, making nothing of him, carrying him back
to the house. I don't know why I followed. Perhaps because
I was at a loose end and suddenly feeling tired.

The woman was bustling about in another room, the old crone was come to life, heating water. Tony took his burden inside and laid him on a cot.

"I feex," he said. "My woman, she feex. You lika drink?"

BACCHUS ALONE KNOWS where he got that stuff or, if he brewed it, of what? It scraped, going down, and it was like liquid fire in my vitals. But it was good. Good as a stimulant for one second and a sedative the next. For a moment I thought I was drugged. Tony's grinning face seemed wreathed in vapor. My own head swam, swelled.

"*Buono* yes? Good when you are tire'. I get you somet'ing to eat while Maria feex heem. Then I get heem somet'ing." He shot a quick look at me. I put the fork of my thumb and forefinger to my nose and sniffed. Tony laughed. He was a scoundrel, but a wholesome rascal at heart. Few of them are rotten throughout.

The mess reeked of garlic, but it was savory, pungent, with spaghetti on the side, I had a long ride ahead of me and then a search, with no beginning, for Kate. My weariness left me as I finished the dish, the dark bread, and wine made from native grapes, he told me.

"Een my country," said Tony, gulping wine, "the women are good for feex the stab, the shot. Who shoot Fin?"

"You'd better ask him," I said diplomatically. It might be awkward if he did, too soon, I reflected, but I had a small arsenal on me. I was not afraid of Tony, after the wolf-dogs. His wife called and he went in.

"I geev heem that coke," he said. "One bullet not een, other one my woman take out, jus' here." He touched a muscle of my shoulder for example. "He not *morto*, this time. He lika speak weeth you before you go."

It would take a little time for the drug to stimulate him, I knew. But I had promised him to get in touch with his mob, send a doctor. Tony's surgery was probably rough and not too likely to be aseptic. I would see Fin through.

His eyes were shining when I went in at last.

"You're a square shooter, guy," he said. "Most would have let me croak. Listen, was you the guy with the jane in Redding's dump? I ain't givin' it away. You don't look like him, but I gotta hunch."

It was a chance I took, a pretty desperate one. Lord knows I had to take many yet ahead. And I had a hunch myself. I accepted the risk.

"You mean the 'scrappin' moll?'"

"I knew it. Some moll! You want to tie to her, guy. She's worth a dozen buddies. So that's how you tied-up with that Fenton lay." His eyes looked puzzled for a minute, but he dismissed his attempt to link things together. "She was there. Billy the Lag twigged her makin' a sneak, see, phonin' the bulls. He goes after her and I cut the wires. We was going to do that anyways. Are you two on the level?"

I nodded.

"You ain't a dick?"

Tony, with true courtesy, had gone out. We were alone.

"Would I have brought you here if I was? I've got no more use for dicks than you have, Fin."

"You got me guessin', guy. Schumann too. Redding wanted you bumped off. I was protectin' him that night, against some other guy he was worryin' over. And that guy got him, after all, through the window. He went up over the roof ahead of me, but I wasn't huntin' him.

"I come in Redding's other door with the key he gave

me, same door the Jap used, and give him the signal. You didn't twig it. There's a pusher taps the bottom of that chair he was in, see. You did me a good turn. Your moil's in Mother Haggerty's. The Chief's to see her to-night."

"Who's he? Where's Mother Haggerty's?"

"I've told you enough, ain't I, for a guy smart enough to do what you've done? That's all, bo'. It's a good tip. If they found out I gave it, it 'ud be curtains fer me. They'd hang a sign on me, see? The coke's wearin' off. I'm tired."

"How about the doctor?" He shook his head. He might have begun to regret what he had said. He was no longer friendly.

"Tony'll look out fer me. On your way, bo'. On your way."

I rode off into the lashing storm, struggling, skidding back to the main road, heading for New York. I took the Mahopac route hoping for better roads. It led close to Ossining's Big House, but that did not bother me. I was done with that.

If there were any road-cops out that stormy night I did not see them and they did not bother me as the four cylinders fought for me and I rushed on, to find Mother Haggerty's—before the Chief saw Kate Wetherill.

8

THIEVES' RENDEZVOUS

I HAVE MET optimistic and confiding people who, despite daily stick-ups and the published accounts of racketeers' fights and the elaborate and expensive funeral rites of gangsters shot down in their cars, firmly believe that the old gangs are a thing of the past—the Gophers and Dusters a mere relic of times that are past, Thieves' Kitchens abolished. These folk are akin to those who think that Prohibition is universally enforced.

It is true that the racketeers live differently these days. They have their apartments on Riverside Drive. The most famous of night club hostesses has said that all gangsters tried to look and live like gentlemen, and gentlemen wanted to be roughnecks. There is some truth in her statement, although her world is limited to a particular cross-section of life.

The modern bravo earns good money. He may protect liquor trucks, or he may be in the employ of hijackers, defend strike-breakers, or go in for bank and mail robbery; but in any case, his price is high. He needs it to live as he wishes. This does not take in the amateurs who stick up drug stores and chain stores, snatch payrolls from a frightened girl in hallways, or grab the returns from an "El" road change-maker. The real gangsters have an aristocracy of their own and regular business organizations.

But there are still places, on the East Side and the West, where the old order is little changed. Even these have their grades of accommodation, and it was to one of the better types of thieves' hang-outs—if the adjective "better" can be rightly employed in such description—that I had to find a way to Mother Haggerty's.

I had to be careful, even if I must be prepared to run many risks. It would be very likely that I would unwittingly ask questions of one who had some affiliations with the Chief's mob, not actively perhaps, but still connected, paying tribute to the gang that protected him. That the Chief had political power went without saying.

Votes are votes, and in the seething cosmopolitanism of Manhattan, with citizens who are still aliens at heart, led by unscrupulous rascals of their own varied races who have learned the tricks of power by pull, offices high and low are won and held by balloting that may be "of the people," but hardly for them.

It arouses the wrath and despair of those who try to do their duty as set down in the vows they take to perform it. Any crime short of murder gets prompt bail, if the criminal has any drag, either in votes or money. The percentage of punishment is small. The swell mobmen laugh at it, though they fear the Baumes Act that sends them up for life after four convictions.

Without doubt the Chief felt himself secure. He and his associates had a swift way of amassing money. In a few months they could acquire what a merchant could not with years of endeavor. If they had sense enough to hold it, invest it, they might retire from the game—but they would always be crooks at heart. I had to be careful of contact with this Chief.

It did not lessen my resolve to dethrone him, to see him properly atone for what he had done or ordered done, to Harvey Pemberton. I could see nothing to balance that score but death for the Chief. I was grimly set upon evening accounts, and I was equally determined not to get entangled in the net of the law.

The resolution obsessed me. It was my life, warped perhaps by it, as Harvey Pemberton's life had been warped. The Chief must be wiped out. For the others, punishment to which death might be preferable, the strippin' from them of their gains, long terms in such places as I had been.

But Kate must first be rescued, and my own affairs were set aside to that end, save as the two efforts coincided. I thought over the men of the underworld I had seen and met at my benefactor's. Harvey Pemberton had helped many of them. They knew his generous side, and numbers took advantage of it. Some might be trusted, and, as I slogged through the night, knowing that every passing minute increased the peril of the girl who had risked so much for me in friendship, I cudgeled my brains to make a choice. At last I came to a decision.

NOW I WAS bound for a certain club, nothing like the After Dark, but one where beggars who sought alms in pity on New York's sidewalks as hopeless cripples appeared miraculously sound after the crowds from whom they made their living had gone home; though of course some of these frauds had night tricks. They are of both sexes, of all colors, these mendicants you see on the streets, huddled in subway entrances and on the stairs of the Elevated. Some are utter failures, degraded by their own weaknesses and appetites. Others are not, possessing comfortable bank accounts, throwing off their misery along with their rags, their sores, their pads and straps; gathering convivially here. And they were graded socially.

It was the place known as "Beggar John's" where I was going, back of the Bowery, looking for "One-Wing" Brady. On his "pitch," not far from the Public Library, Brady plies his trade, licensed, offering pencils to comply with the law, represented by officers who pass him by, save when they collect their graft. One sleeve, the right, hangs empty, save for a protruding stump that, with the cleverly arranged padding, conceals the fact that Brady has his real "wing" deftly strapped down beneath his shirt. He has his patter, his melancholy visage. He acts one role for a continuous run, and he is perfect in the part.

Once he was close to dying. Appendicitis he stubbornly fought off, then pneumonia. He was robbed, and Harvey Pemberton came to his rescue. He swore gratitude. I had to chance its being genuine. But he knew his New York. I knew much of it, but I had never heard of Mother Haggerty. If Brady did not know, would not tell me— I would not consider that.

It stopped raining as I guided my motorcycle onto the Bronx Park Fairway, the gale blown inside out. Now it was cold, and I was soaked to the bone, it seemed. Under the lights I recognized what a strange figure I cut, and I discarded my torn overalls and left them in shrubbery to furnish a mystery for aspiring dicks, with the bloodstains that, since I had handled Fin, were human as well

as canine. I had left my rag of a wig elsewhere. My hair
was long enough to pass muster. Under my sopping cap it
lay slicked down.

In my knickers and sports coat I looked sufficiently
forlorn, but I might be only some foolhardy holiday-maker
caught by the storm, making for home. A traffic sign held
me, high uptown. I passed the line by a slight margin before
it flashed and backed up. The traffic cop blew his whistle,
looked at me, and came over.

"Let's see what you've got in that side-car," he said. "It
ain't a passenger."

"Think I'd let my girl friend ride a night like this. Took
my last dollar to put her on the train. There's nothing in
it. Take a look."

"I'm going to," he said. "Where do you live?"

I gave him an address on Perry Street in Greenwich
Village. He glanced in the side-car, drawing aside the wind
curtain with its celluloid window, then again at me. If he
asked me for my license I was going to be held up. It should
be only a "ticket," but Fin's blood was on the cushions of
the side-car. He might make a more thorough search. I
was carrying unlawful weapons. But he looked me over,
bedraggled in my sports clothes, and laughed.

"A Villager, eh? Get along with you. The makeup passes
you."

He thought I was some more or less eccentric artist or
writer, to his ideas a little cracked. His sense of humor, half
derisive, half friendly, saw me through.

It seemed to me I would never get down town. I swung
off to the west, and then abandoned that idea because of
the tough going on bad streets. New York, as ever, was

being torn up and undermined. There were hollows that threw me in the air, cobbles that threatened to jolt the cycle apart, while the side-car leaped beside me.

IT SEEMED AS if a full day, at least, measured by hours, had passed since I set out; but when at last I got through to Madison Square the light showed on top of the Metropolitan Tower and it was only chiming midnight. Only! The thought of what might have happened made me desperate, yet it was probable that night, to the Chief, was the business day. I was fairly sure that Schumann had gone to meet him, to deliver the swag. That would take time. He was probably business man enough to delay interviewing his captive until his leisure, getting a perverted pleasure out of it.

My body needed sleep, but I could do without it. Under stress a man can get along if spurred by earnest purpose. Vitality needs fuel to maintain reserves and I was thankful for that meal of Tony's. I could have done with another drink. It is often a poor enough crutch, but there are times when it goes direct to prime flagging automatic human mechanism.

It was not easy to get into Beggar John's. I did not look as if I belonged to the fraternity though I looked, tough enough, wet, spattered with mud. The "club" was in the basement, and a man surveyed me with open suspicion through a grille in the doorway. He probably thought I was trying to crash the gate for some liquor.

"This ain't a speakeasy," he growled. But I got the name "One-Wing" to him before he closed the little shutter, and he paused. He caught sight of a bill in my hand.

"What youse want wit' One-Wing?"

"Tell him it's the Kid."

He looked at me again, considered, grabbed the five dollars and went down a passage. One-Wing knew I was "out." He would remember the moniker the underworld visitors to my foster-father's had bestowed upon me. I had put myself in his power. But I did not think he was a "stool," to give me up for a reward. If he thought I had money he might blackmail me. There are plenty of men out of a penitentiary after having served their terms, trying to live it down, who are hunted for years by other prisoners, and by guards, levying "come-through" money, keeping track of them.

As the minutes passed and I waited in that dirty areaway I began to think the worst, but the man came back and let me in. I heard laughter, music from a radio, a medley of voices as a door opened at the far end of a passage and One-Wing, peering at me in the dim light, came forward. He did not know me, naturally enough, adept on make-up as he was; until I spoke.

"Get in the office, Kid," he said and piloted me into a small room that had a desk and a telephone, two or three chairs, some used newspapers lying on a table.

"It's O.K., Stumpy," he said to the guardian of the grille. "'S the Kid I know."

He said nothing about my changed appearance, nothing about my escape. He was essentially wise.

"What can I do for you?" he asked.

"How far would you go?" I queried. If he gave me the information I wanted it might put him in wrong enough. I knew that. But I was not going to require too much of him. With Billings, the peterman, who had rendered me one service at Redding's, I was content. It was not fair to want more from one man. Billings had gone to Washington, or I might even so have asked him about Mother Haggerty.

"All the way, Kid."

BUT HIS FACE changed when I mentioned what I was after. His eyes showed a certain dread.

"I can tip you off to Mother Haggerty," he said, "but you want to leave the Chief alone, Kid. You'll git into trouble. Better forgit it. He may have had something to do with a certain job you're thinkin' of but he can't be touched."

"This has got to do with a girl. I owe her a lot. She means a lot to me."

"Kid, you leave the janes alone. They're too risky. Windmills. Never know when they're goin' to turn. You ain't in a position to monkey with 'em."

"She's at Mother Haggerty's. The Chief's got her."

"Then Gord help her," said One-Wing, solemnly.

"I've got to get her out. She's in trouble, on my account. She's not our sort, One-Wing." He sniffed at that.

"They're all the same. You look as if you'd been through hell, Kid."

"I have. Still in it."

"I said I'll go all the way. All right, I'll do it, but it may be the last of you as well as the girl. The Chief's bad medicine. Stands in strong. I know something about him and there's a lot I don't know—and don't want to. Some say he's some sort of wop. They say he was with Villa in Mexico. Ran contraband over the line afterwards. Chinese, and dope. Then he came to New York and got in the Big Game. Right. Some call him *El Capitán*, or did. Greaser or half-breed probably. Cold-blooded as sin. Head of a big mob and works under cover. At that I reckon they know him at Headquarters but they've got nothing on him, or don't want to have. When a dick can draw down twenty times his pay for bein' blind and dumb, you can guess what often happens."

He was talking naturally, unconscious of cynicism.

"He'll be at Haggerty's to-night. This morning," I said. "I've got to hurry."

"You're hurryin' to knock on hell's front door, Kid. But you're set fer it. Mother Haggerty runs a boarding house, quite respectable. Brown Front. West Thirties. Here's the address fer you."

He wrote it down on the desk and handed it to me. I read it, burned it as he nodded approval.

"She's no good. Never was. Her lodgers are all grifters and travelin' men. I guess the Chief covers her."

I knew what he meant. Men who plied confidence games, blackmail, others who went out of town on "jobs."

"She's a stool. They ain't got it on her yet, but some day a guy'll come out of the Big House and they'll find her with her throat cut. But she's boss in her house. You'd think they were all regular drummers. And she sees they don't run out on her. Those that tried it got theirs. Because she stands in with the Chief, mebbe they figure he turns 'em in. She wouldn't dare stool on *him*. She knows what would happen to her, the old she-devil! She's got plenty on him. Your jane ain't the first girl she's looked after fer, on the Chief's account."

ALL THIS TALK was in the thief's whisper. Half the time I read his lips. He was afraid, badly, but he was game, and

grateful. Harvey Pemberton's breed was coming back from
the dark water over which he had gone.

"If the Chief's there, you'll never get in to her. You
wouldn't if he was even expected but fer one thing. She'll
have the girl in her own apartment.

"It is one flight up. I've been there. She's got one weak
spot. I don't give her credit fer it. She never done a thing
to be give credit fer."

A bell rang and he spoke out louder, glibly shifting the
topic, as the guard went down the passage.

"That sure sounds fine, Kid. I'm glad you made it. When
do you leave?"

"To-morrow," I played up. "It looks like a good thing. I
thought you'd be able to tell me something about it."

The newcomer was admitted. The footsteps passed.
One-Wing went on.

"I'll bet she was a rotten mother, though you can't tell.
A woman 'll do anything fer her kids and think she's justified. Built that way. Meant to be, mebbe. Anyway, her boy
is missin' and she's never quit tryin' to find him. Advertised
all over the world. He was no good. No nerve. A natural
squealer. It's a cinch the little rat was bumped off, long ago.
But she don't believe it. They bleed her all the time with
fake news. You tell her you've got word of young Bob and
she'll let you in, if the Chief ain't there. She's got his picture
on her mantelpiece in a silver frame. There's a man inside
here got a description of him, printed. I'll git it from him,
an' somethin' else. He's O.K. I'm leary about this fer myself
as well as you, Kid. I'm doin' fine since you-know-who put
me on my feet."

He knew he was skating on thin ice. I had to have young

Bob's description. I made up a plausible tale to pitch to
her while I waited for him. It seemed an hour that he was
gone, but it was less than five minutes. He gave me the
dirty handbill and I read it through, every word fixed on
my mind, with the picture at the top of a gangling runt,
evil and cowardice stamped on his features. Rat eyes and
no chin, a broken nose. The description was a good one,
down to body marks, scars and tattoos.

"If trouble starts in that dump, Kid," said One-Wing,
"you look out. If they figure you as an outsider you'll be
one. And you won't go out on your feet. They'd do it quiet.
She don't like shootin'. But I'll bet she's got 'drops' in her
cupboard, and others have got blackjacks. It's up to you. If
you don't get your jane away before the Chief comes, look
out. When they called him *El Capitán* he packed a knife,
and he will now. But I got this for you. You squeeze this in
front of a guy's nose and he's out. In a breath. We call it the
'knock.' It's methyl or ethyl something or other."

It was a gelatine capsule nearly filled with fluid, such as
they use for certain unpalatable medicines. I started to put
it in my pocket when he checked me.

"You can't show up the way you are," he said. "Got any
money? Then we'll go to Lazarus. Almost next door. He's
always open for cash. Keeps his mouth shut under that
long nose of his and he can fix you up."

9

MOTHER HAGGERTY'S

MORE DELAY, IT meant; but it was sound advice enough.
I looked like a scarecrow. I could do without shaving, but
I had to get clean and presentable if I hoped to break
through to Mother Haggerty. One-Wing told me I need
have no fear of her not being up. She was a nighthawk,
sleeping as her lodgers did till noon. And he reassured
me a little about the Chief—*El Capitán*—the "Cap" of
Redding's notebook New York never sleeps. Some work
double shifts; to many, day is for slumber.

Lazarus looked dubious until he caught sight of money,
knew I had come to buy instead of to sell and exchange.
He moved fast enough and I got a flashy suit that fitted
fairly well, a shirt, collar and tie, a soft hat and a raincoat.
Not at a bargain for me, but he scented one, and money
to me was only chips shoved into the game I was playing.

He let me park my motorcycle in a room at the back
which had held many a questionable object; did now, I did
not doubt, nor care. I took along one gun.

One I traded for the raincoat and the third I gave to
One-Wing. We parted on the street and I went to look for
a cab, he returning to his "club," his last words in my ears:

"You're sittin' in a game where it's all stacked against you.
Don't forget the 'knock.'"

I paid my driver off at the corner and walked down the
street. Two men entered the respectable brownstone front
I found to be hers. The name on the slip of card over her
bell in neat printing:

Mrs. Eliza M. Haggerty

I rang, took down the little tube transmitter and heard a
hard voice, high and feminine, tell me in the same breath
she could see no one and ask who I was and my business.
The Chief, I fancied, would come in with his own key.

I have never seen a more vulpine, avaricious, discon-
tented face. It was not scored so much by indulgence as
by the nature of the woman, evil, secretive, treacherous,
revealing her inner self.

Physiognomy may often be misleading, but even a child
would have mistrusted her. Her eyes were stony as she
admitted me to her front room. Her face as hard, uncom-
promising. One-Wing had called her a she-devil and I
thought him not far out.

"You say you've news about my boy?" she snapped and I
noticed there was no picture on the mantel. "I don't want
any second-hand stuff. If you've seen him and talked with
him, or if you've got letters from him that ain't fakes, I'll
talk with you, though I'm expecting some one else. When
he comes, you clear out. I may see you later."

My pulse went up a beat or two. The Chief had not
arrived! I took care not to glance about the room, but there
was not much I missed. A door led into a dining room.

There was probably a kitchenette off that. Beyond, one or more rooms.

"I'm his mother but I'm through being fooled," she went on sharply. "I've had too many bums lying to me to cadge a few dollars, looking at the picture I was fool enough to have on exhibition, and trying to describe him. Some of 'em got hold of some dodgers I had sent out. But *you* can't fool me, young man.

"Tell me, what's your line? When did you come to New York?"

"Four days ago," I lied easily. When you play against crooked cards you must mark your own. I had no sympathy for her, even aside from what One-Wing said about her. She was holding Kate, within twenty or thirty feet of me, she was a panderer to the Chief, she had no decency or scruples.

In a minute or two I might have to fight her. But I kept out of my eyes what I felt.

"I make a good spiel," I told her. That was a phrase that might mean side-show connections or many other things; just what a cagy grifter in a get-up like mine would use. "Bob gave me your address, but I was busy. He said there was a reward out for him."

"Then why don't he come back or write himself? It don't look like you'll collect any money. You'd better clear out. When did you get out of jail?"

IT WAS A taunt rather than intuition. It was startling, but I grinned at her. It was my talk rather than my appearance that justified the fling.

"I don't want your kale," I said. "I've got my own. Plenty. I came here on the cushions—from Colorado. Your boy's in Cañon City. There are good reasons why he don't write or come. They won't let him."

"The Pen?" For just a moment she showed a human reaction. "What's he in for?" she asked.

"You wouldn't want to know. Good night, lady. I came here to do you a good turn and because I told him I would. I was there too. Fer sellin' bum minin' stock. I was a trusty, see? He won't ever be."

"What's he in for?" She gripped my arm. It was what I wanted. I had placed my long gabardine raincoat over the back of a chair. Turning, as if to wrench loose and go, I flung it over her head and muffled her in it, none too gently, bore her kicking and fighting like a wild cat to a davenport lounge, and tied her up with "safety"—insulated wire I had got from Lazarus, who did not profess to deal in electric sundries, but had a varied stock of useful commodities to suit his trade.

She struggled hard, being bony and surprisingly strong, but I gave her no chance. She was the sort who does not faint, but who will fake. If she was knocked out, the first thing she would do, recovering consciousness, would be to yell. And she had a house full of men who would, for their own sakes, get rid of any stranger who was pulling strong-arm stuff. I stuffed her mouth with cotton, crisscrossed it with adhesive tape, all from the accommodating Lazarus; then I rolled her back of her davenport, partly under it.

I set the room in order, started for the back of the apartment and heard the slight click of the door to the hall. A man came into the room, dressed with scrupulous care in dinner clothes, his coat open, showing the gleam of one cabochon ruby in his soft, finely pleated shirt. It looked like a drop of blood. He carried a cloak, richly lined with satin, over his arm, and tossed it to a chair.

The "Chief!" *El Capitán!* No other. Mexican, or Spanish, I rated him. Sleek as a tiger and with the eyes of one, a supple, lean body. A fighting man who liked to kill—and who liked first to torture. He carried gloves in one hand and leaned lightly on a slim malacca cane that looked like an over-long swagger stick. A soft black hat on his head.

"So," he said softly in flawless English, "what the devil are you doing here, and where is Mrs. Haggerty? Keep your hand out of your pocket, my friend, or I'll run you through."

Lazarus had played a dirty trick on me, after all, without intent. The suit I had bought from him, turned in by some down-on-his-luck mobman, had been silk-lined. I had seen that was worn and a little frayed, but I had not noticed that the stouter sateen in the right-hand pocket had a hole in it. My gun-sight caught in it, clogged the draw. I could not even level it to shoot through the cloth.

He had whipped out from his cane a triangular blade. He held the hollow casing of the sword-cane in one hand and made the steel whizz as he brought it, with a flourish, pointing at me. Not at my breast, but lower.

"I shall run you through the belly," he said, "if you make a move. Answer my question."

There was no chance for the "knock." The man was agile as a fencing master. He could strike with the scabbard or spit me with the sword, as he chose. I knew a little Spanish. I had to surprise him, get him off guard somehow.

"*Yo no sé, señor,*" I answered, and saw his eyes narrow, glittering, still on guard, ready for a lightning move, but puzzled. "I don't know. I came to see her about her kid,

see? She went into the other room, what for I don't know.
You've got no call to make a play like that. I told her the
straight goods, and she's paying me for it."

He did not glance aside.

"**WHAT DID YOU** tell her? That he is dead?"

"*Seguramente,*" I said, banking on One-Wing's estimate
of the rat. "Sure."

"When and where, my Mexican-speaking friend? You
seem to know who I am. I shall know you again, but it will
not matter. If you have lied to her, it is going to be very
unfortunate for you. *Muy malo,* Señor Moocher."

He took me for a race-tout who had been to Tia Juana.
But I had a nasty feeling that this was my finish. Evidently
he knew all about Bob Haggerty.

"Ah!" His eyes flashed, opened wide. Mother Haggerty
had managed somehow to shift the davenport with her
knees. And, for a split-second, he looked that way.

I dropped backward on hands and elbows and launched
a double kick at him as his blade scored my scalp with his
lunge and stuck in the flooring. I got him on both knees
with nerve-shattering force and leaped for him as he went
staggering back. He struck at me with the cane-case and
broke it over my head and shoulders. I barely felt the blows.
I had him down now, and we rolled, fighting to be top dog.
I suppose he was too proud to cry out, to have others see
him down. He was clever, but he was vain, with a touch of
the theatrical, as his clothes suggested, always playing the
star role, hero to himself.

And he was powerful. If Mother Haggerty, struggling
back of the davenport to get free, to rid herself of her gag,

had fought like a wild cat, I now had a human jaguar on my hands.

I am no slouch. The time on Long Island had gone far to keep me in shape. I had a little the better of him in weight, and I put out my full strength in continuous effort. But he was built up of bone and rubber and steel. Alternately he relaxed and made dynamic bursts of furious attack.

He fought like a Mexican bandit, using or trying to use every foul trick he knew, a full catalogue. He tried to gouge out my eyes, and got his thumb hooked into one before I tore away. He used his knees, his teeth and nails, and I had to match him at his own dirty game. We were fighting for life. And I for Kate, besides myself.

He slugged me behind my ear and almost stunned me. I hit where I could with hard jolts. Once I smashed his mouth, and split his lips, and my knuckles barked against his teeth, but I tried hardest for his body. A short jab to his liver hurt him, and he grunted, cursed through his swelling mouth in Mexican. I knew he had a knife somewhere, was playing all the time to get it.

A chair fell over, but it was a flimsy thing, and the rug was thick and soft. We were both panting, but no one had heard us, aside from the woman who was flurrying uselessly. I had my hands on his throat, but he brought up a blow to my chin that almost put me out, almost numbed my brain to danger.

My hold weakened, and he got to his feet. He was too wary to try for his sword again, but a knife flashed from the back of his belt. With a prodigious effort, nerved by thought of the girl who would be at his mercy, I found footing and gripped his right wrist, side-stepping, my left arm back of his elbow, left hand on his chest where the shirt was ripped open, the ruby gone.

I meant to break his arm. I was too weak for that, for the moment, but I hurt him so badly that he dropped the knife. My gun was still entangled, the lining worse torn. I had badly bruised my hip as we wrestled. Now, gasping for wind, I put all I had into a swing for his jaw.

It seemed to glance off, but he fell in a heap and for the moment I stood half stupid, swaying, thinking I had won, until I saw his strategy, to get back his knife. But he was far from his best. I got him from behind, shutting off his breath and voice, sinking my fingers about his windpipe, seeking the jugular, my thumb on it as his breath wheezed and rattled in his throat and his olive skin turned purple.

HE COLLAPSED IN earnest, and I knelt over him, myself almost done, like a fighter taking the count I sorely needed. He was out this time, choked almost to death. I have wished since that I had finished him. But I fancied I heard some one listening outside the door, stealthy steps and voices. I shot the bolt.

I had used all my insulated wire on the woman, but I took the cords that held back the draperies on the front windows. I plastered his mouth, leaving him to breathe as best he could through his nose. I took a look at Mother Haggerty and saw surely the face of Satan's wife glaring up at me.

Beyond the dining room with its kitchenette was a bedroom. Beyond that another room, with the key in the door, two bolts shot, on this side. Swiftly I released them and found some one clinging to the handle on the other side.

"Kate!" I cried softly. "Let me in."

No need to tell her my name. I heard her sigh of relief and found her in a room with barred windows and fastened casements. She was in her torn evening gown. I hurried back to the front room to get my raincoat for her, and, not seeing it at once, snatched at the cloak of *El Capitán*. He was breathing stertorously, but still lay limp.

There was some one knocking at the door. Those footsteps I had heard with the voices were real. I could not masquerade as the Chief. Kate's dishevelment needed covering more than mine.

She looked what she was, a prisoner seeking to escape.

I had my gun free now, but we would have to fight our way down and out.

The knocking grew louder, more impatient, drumming like a tambour of misfortune.

Kate had followed me, gazing at *El Capitán*, who was beginning to stir, and at the shifting davenport.

"The other door," I whispered. There was not only the one door of communication to her back prison, but another from the Haggerty woman's bedroom to the hall.

I looked into the little kitchenette, saw what I wanted on the shelves. Two cans. Pepper, white and red. I opened them and filled my left palm with the mixture.

"Open the door when I tell you," I said, meaning to go out gun first. She asked for a handful of the pepper, then helped herself.

The old-fashioned stairs headed in front with two turns for the flight. There might be danger above as well as below. I was going down to the street.

There were four men outside that door, one in a dressing

gown, the rest in shirt sleeves. They were debating; whether in knowledge of the Chief's being there, I could not tell. Two were pounding on the panels. A hard, cold-featured bunch. There were no guns in sight. We might surprise them, get down to the ground floor. They might have come from there; but at any moment others might join them.

SUDDENLY THERE WAS a stifled shout. The Chief's bloody lips must have loosened the plaster on his mouth. Two men whipped out blackjacks, and the pair who had been knocking set their shoulders to the door. And then a yell came from above. People had been looking over the banisters and had seen us, back of the half-opened door.

"Come," I said, and we made for the head of the stairs, I in front of Kate, as I thought, though there was no more safety in the rear with the rush that started.

They swerved at sight of my gun, but one swerved, dodged, blackjack in hand, to fall back, crouching, covering his face, blinded with the pepper Kate had flung full in his face. I let them have my charge and left two sneezing, groping, while my gun barrel felled the fourth and we gained the stairs.

The hall was vacant, but the front door had combination latches. I fumbled with them, one-handed, and gave way to Kate, turning to meet the rest who came charging down.

I did not want to fire if I could help it; in that house, that smug neighborhood, that might harbor others of their kind. An alarm like that might involve us with the law, and in that precinct the word of *El Capitán* might go far. It was a sinister and suggestive thing that they did not fire at us. Sinister and cautious.

The locks were cleverly planned to balk one not used to

them. Kate worked at them steadily, half breathless from her flight and the excitement. She had been in an unventilated room, half fed, unable to eat. But she was game, dead game. If I ever got her out of this she must stay clear of me. That thought flashed clear in my mind, for all the peril of the moment.

The door by which I stood, a parlor suite, swung inward. A great arm shot out and a hairy hand grasped my gun wrist, grinding bones and flesh together as I turned and wrestled with a giant of a man in pyjamas, the upper garment open, showing his massive, matted chest. I cried to Kate to go, while she still struggled with the stubborn locks and the men came leaping down upon us.

10

PLIGHT

I SUPPOSE I had been badly jarred. I knew now that I had little strength left, which was hardly to be wondered at. But the door was open at last and Kate was fighting the big brute who held me. She bit at his wrist, sobbing, and I got one hand free. I had dropped the gun. That hand was out of commission.

The "knock!" I fumbled in my vest pocket while the girl's attack still worried him. I found the capsule, got it out and thrust it in his leering face, crushing it. It was elastic but brittle too, with force enough applied. It broke beneath his nose and the effect was instantaneous.

His eyes widened, glazed. He let loose of me and fell back with a crash. We were through the door, slamming it in the faces of that slavering mob coming down the stairs. I had no doubt they would be after us, *El Capitán*, released by now, would be furiously active.

By the good grace of Heaven, as I then thought, there was a taxicab across the street. The engine was running, the driver standing facing the house, and us, as we bolted for the seeming refuge. He opened the door and we jumped in as he jammed in the gears to the quick getaway of a Manhattan nighthawk chauffeur.

I glimpsed the Haggerty door opening. As we swung a corner I saw a patrolman running down the sidewalk, pounding his nightstick on it. We were going fast, but not too fast, though, as we turned again, our man gave it full gas. He was our *deus ex machina*, the god from the machine, and we were in it.

We went dodging across town and suddenly turned into an all-night garage whose doors opened to his honk, closed after us.

"Clean getaway!" he said. "I'll take you where you want to go, soon as I've changed back to my right license plates. The guy who runs this joint is a friend of mine—and Brady's," he added with a wink.

"One-Wing?"

"That's his business moniker. He got in touch with me and told me to stall around near that house, see, in case some friends of his, a gent and a lady, should want a cab in a hurry. So there I was, and it seemed like something was goin' to break. That dump ain't what you'd call a safety station, mister."

One-Wing had said he would go all the way. He had gone far, already.

"IT MIGHT BE best if I left my cab here for the night," he said. "Bill will loan me a private machine. He's got 'em handy." He winked again, good naturedly. I guessed that Bill did business in used cars whose original part-numbers were no longer theirs. It was none of my affair, save to see Bill paid for his loaned car.

"That cuts you out of your night trade," I said to the driver, "but I'll make it up to you."

"Now or never, boss," he answered cheerfully. "Brady

said you might be short and I told him to forgit it. Where can I take you?"

I looked at Kate, pale now, tired.

"Home," she said. "To my own place. Come with me, Paul. I can get something to eat there though it seems banal to talk of eating. But I'm half starved. You look a wreck."

I was. My clothes had lost buttons from coat and vest. I had no hat and I had left my raincoat at Mother Haggerty's, souvenirs I was quite sure even *El Capitán* could not trace. Lazarus was too old at his own game. There was a smear of blood on my forehead and my hair was stiff from the scrape of the sword-cane. My body ached infernally and I wanted to get to bed. I wasn't going back to Long Island. I still had a latch-key to my friend's apartment that he had insisted on my keeping for emergency; I could go there later. Friends are the gifts of the gods.

"I'll go with you this once," I said. "I can eat also. And I've got to have a talk with you."

"You've not had enough? Poor Paul!"

"No," I said savagely. The caress in her voice was destructive. "But there is a lot to talk over. You've got to explain your reappearance."

"I'll say that I was kidnaped," she said. "Taken to a lonely place in the country. And I bribed my way out, if you want to forego the part of hero. I don't know who took me. Can't even describe them properly."

It was as good a story as any that her quick wit evolved. We could polish it presently.

"Want to wash up, boss? Don't want to butt in. Shall I borrow a sedan?"

He let go and fell back with a crash

"Fine," I told him. "And give this to Bill. This is for you, outside what we'll owe you later."

He glowed at sight of the two fifties I peeled off.

"I know a gent when I see one," he said. "You don't owe me nothin'."

I washed my face and hands at a standing sink with Kate beside me and then the sedan was ready.

I pretended to doze on that ride though I knew she was looking at me commiseratingly. Yet she had shown spirit that might understand something of my resolve. We had both gone back to the primitive.

The dignified street was quiet. We had left all alarm behind. Our driver steadfastly refused to accept anything, but he gave me his name and where he could be found.

"Any time you want a chap that knows his apples," he said, "get in touch with me there, or at Bill's. Good night and good luck."

"I WONDER WHAT he thinks of us," said Kate as we went in past a respectful doorman, who seemed to purposely ignore my clothes.

"You look like a gunman, Paul."

"I've been using one," I replied grimly. I did not intend to tell her my day's exploits in full. "If you mean the driver, he's seen stranger things and he's a friend of a friend of mine."

"The doorman's a friend of mine," she said. "He won't even look at you when you go out. You needn't worry about Barney. I got him the job."

It was an automatic elevator and soon we were in her apartment. Maid service came from the house. We were alone. I was a bizarre figure in those rooms as I caught a glimpse of myself before I sank down in a great chair, while Kate excused herself. I fell asleep at once.

She was close to me when I woke with a start and her face was a little flushed.

She had put on a negligee and brought in a tray.

She said it was not much. I don't know what I ate, save that it was a far different meal from that at Tony's. A far cry from here to that farmhouse where Fin lay feverish, repenting perhaps, of what he had told me.

There was wine, I remember that. It put a tingle into me. Coffee fresh from an electric percolator. Salad, I think, and cold chicken. I forced myself to help her to go over what she must say to the Fentons when she called them later. The hue and cry must be stopped. There would be reporters to see.

"It's got to be the end of all this," I said sternly.

"The end—of what?" she asked softly. "Everything?"

"There is no end to friendship, I suppose," I hedged. "It's radioactive. But this is the end of your life crossing mine. I'm an outlaw; beyond law, and there is nothing ahead for me but the sort of thing I have exposed you to. It must finish."

"*You* did not call *me* on the telephone that night—was it the night before last? I've lost count of time."

"It makes no difference. Promise me."

She shook her head, drooping a little.

"Promises are dangerous things, Paul. I'll try to do what you want."

"I'll help you," I replied. "I'm going."

"Where?"

"To a safe place where I can sleep. I need it. Good night—and good-by, Kate."

"Good night."

For all the stress of the whole affair, I was like a man walking in my sleep. The next thing I knew I was in a cab. My friend's rooms were vacant. There was a note on the sideboard.

"Gone to Philly. Back on the eighteenth. Help yourself."

He enters no more into my story. Let him be nameless. He is still my friend.

11

LAYING A TRAP

THE FIRST THING I glimpsed when I woke up, with the light pouring in through the window, pale but brilliant winter sunshine, was the cloak of *El Capitán*, hanging over the foot of the bed, its black satin lining resplendent. I had, of course, brought it from Kate's, but my physical actions had been largely automatic. I had no recollection of bringing it, and for a few seconds I had some difficulty in getting things together at all in my mind.

As for my body, it was stiff as that of a player after a hard football game, who goes home without a rubdown. The top of my head was tender. *El Capitán* had ripped the scalp with the point of that confounded sword-cane of his. I was bruised slightly on the face, more on the body, sore where the entangled gun had ground into my hip. It was the jolting ride in the pouring rain that had contributed most to my condition, I imagined, but there was little that a Turkish bath would not get rid of.

For a while I lay there, piecing things together. All in all, I had surely been lucky. If Mother Haggerty had not managed to shift that davenport I would now be in a sewer, or at the bottom of the East River, with a bag of scrap-iron holding me down—run through the belly, and the heart

to finish it And there were a few other times earlier where
the breaks had been in my favor.

Reason mounted its pulpit and began to preach to me
the folly of attempting this revenge of mine single-handed.
I had friends, but I was going to need actual and active
followers, a mob of my own I could depend upon. Sooner
or later *El Capitán* was going to take the offensive. He had
said, very distinctly, that he would know me again. And,
if he ever caught sight of me, he was going to do his best
not to lose me.

So said Reason. But I didn't see where I was going to
enlist my henchmen unless I hired professional gunmen;
and the idea of a personal vengeance still clung to me. I
had friends, but I did not wish to involve them too deeply.

El Capitán—that title was far more suitable for him than
"Chief"—had been humiliated, bested in a man-to-man
encounter. He was not the kind who likes to crawl out of
the small end of the horn. The theatrical vanity of the chap
was manifest in that soft pleated shirt, the soft hat, the
cabochon ruby and the matador effect of the hair, close-
trimmed, that he wore in front of his ears. And the cloak!
You don't see many such cloaks. Occasionally a flamboyant
artist wears one.

El Capitán was a master-bravo. He loved to dress the
part, to show himself, as he fancied, a *caballero, hidalgo,* one
of the *fina genie.*

No doubt he had some good blood in his veins. He was
not only unscrupulous but highly intelligent, or he could
not have led the mob he did. He found in New York much
the same opportunity as lies in Mexico for the bribery of
officials whose pay is not adequate to the times in which

they live. A patrolman sees money spent right and left, and presently it is offered to him to keep his eyes shut or turned the other way. And that goes straight up the line. The number of defaulters in financial institutions mounts daily. The bench itself is not immune. It was an atmosphere in which *El Capitán* was quite at home.

From helping to command the irregulars of Villa, bandits all, he had turned *contrabandista,* smuggler. Now he had advanced to the rank of master-robber in the city where the opportunities were greatest. He had planned the ring of seemingly reputable merchants who were master fences. The bandits had been replaced by men who robbed lofts, jewelers, and places like Fenton's where a big haul could be made. Supplemented by gangster gunmen.

The loot would pass through the apparently legitimate hands of Bowerman, general merchandise broker; Mallet, specializing in woolen goods; Schumann, who looked after the gems. Lee I could not place. He might handle any negotiable paper, stocks and bonds, they annexed. I did not fancy that they bothered with banks, pay rolls, or mail trains. But it was more than probable that they had something to do with the goods missing from freight cars when they arrived at their destination in New York.

It was a well laid out scheme. I imagined that the robberies were not undertaken without being ratified by *El Capitán* and his four associates—five, when Redding was alive. Redding, I was practically certain, had been found lacking and had been eliminated, even though he had Fin to protect him that night. Fin might not have known of the decision to "hang a sign" on Redding or that the orders were given. Though it might only be that Redding's private life had made him a target for assassination.

EVERYTHING SHOWED *EL CAPITÁN* as a picaresque genius, a superscamp. Your " 'breed" is generally dangerous, usually credited—or discredited—with having all the vices and none of the virtues of the races that intermingle in him. Often the blood is impure on both sides; but when it is not, when your 'breed has brains that are devoted to villainy, he is a sinister character, leaning to the picturesque, inclined to the medieval in his personal ways, but quick enough to take full advantage of modern conditions. After all, bribery is as old as man.

He would be on the lookout for me. Fin evidently had not been in touch with him personally, but he must have talked. In this game, as in chess, one must be careful of the openings, looking many moves ahead to study his opponent's strategy. I had to accept the probability, that *El Capitán* believed that, in his possession of the girl, he had a clew to the man who had gone to Redding's rooms and who had later returned and got hold of Redding's private records, taking some of them that might be dynamite where he and his ring were concerned.

I did not know, of course, whether the man who had opened Redding's safe and was examining the wallet and notebook when Billings blackjacked him with the cane had recognized just what it contained. The odds were that he had, that he had been told to look for some such record. A proper rascal himself, *El Capitán* would have sensed what Redding might be up to, thinking he was protecting himself—a dogfish among sharks.

They would be desperate to get that back. They would be

apt to think that I was either Richard Pemberton himself
who had gone after Redding, or some one he had commis-
sioned. I had never met *El Capitán* or any of the mob
save Redding in my foster-father's house. *El Capitán* had
certainly not known who I was at Mother Haggerty's.
Schumann did not even know what I looked like in my
cap and goggles, my nondescript overall. But they were
shrewd. What with Fin, who was out of the way for a
while as an active member, but who would soon get in
touch with them, they would be looking for the man who
had come to the rescue of Kate Wetherill, the pawn they
had won and lost.

I had taken chances, I suppose I had left loopholes, but
the game had moved swiftly and been complicated by the
necessity of getting her clear. Now I must go softly, very
softly. The Italians have a proverb that he who goes *pianis-*
simo, goes wisely, and arrives. Paul Standing could never
be identified legally as Richard Pemberton unless they got
hold of Blessing, the facial surgeon, and I knew that he
would never divulge anything about me.

It came down to this, that *El Capitán* would have to
see me as Paul Standing and have me shadowed, disposed
of. Fin had seen me without my goggles, but my features
had been masked with mud. He had seen me at Redding's
before my features were changed, and at that time I had
worn a dark wig. I was uncertain about Fin. His gratitude
might have passed. But I felt fairly safe unless they got hold
of Randall and tied me up with the phone call when Kate
had warned me of the robbery at Fenton's. It was a complicated coil and took some thinking to clarify it.

I might get my features changed again and use still

another name, but my pride revolted against that. I had a streak of the melodramatic in me, as well as *El Capitán*. He would not disguise himself, I fancied, though I did not know his name or where he lived. To change my identity once more would fortify my position in cutting myself off with Kate. That might have had something to do with my decision to remain as I was. We all have our weaknesses, our spots of deliberate blindness.

To cope successfully with rogues who know no limit, one should be ruthless. I should not have left alive the man we had found by Redding's open safe. But I did not want to kill, with the exception of *El Capitán*. He was the potential murderer of my benefactor, if not the actual. Yet I wanted to do that in open fight. It would have been better if I had not had any scruples, automatic as they had been, at Mother Haggerty's—if I had killed him while my fingers were round his throat. I think only the knocking at the door, the urgent need to get to Kate, saved him then.

I MEANT TO see that punishment was meted out to the others, through the law, through my efforts. And I had the plan ready for the demolition of Schumann, with only one flaw in it. It involved a personal appearance and *El Capitán* might well have described me and warned him.

That could be overcome in only one way. I would have to use a temporary disguise, after all. I did not think that Schumann had been so upset as to resolve to close up his offices on Nassau Street, give up his source of riches, and destroy his usefulness. *El Capitán* would stiffen him there. I fancied that, while he was suspicious, he would only consider me a gangster who had been tipped off and was after the Fenton loot, merely as loot. A hi-jacker. That illusion would not hold long. Fin would be likely to explode that, aside from the Randall possibility. But it would take time. With the right disguise I could hook Schumann.

Aching, I got out of bed and took a hot bath. I rang up the clothing store I had previously patronized, gave my measures and instructions to send up some clothes immediately. Two suits, one a plain, conservative business suit. Other things including a hat and kit bag. Then I reserved quarters at a quiet bachelor hotel I knew. I shaved, wincingly dressed the shallow groove in my scalp and arranged my hair, putting on a dressing robe I found in a closet, writing a note for my friend that I was not returning to Long Island and asking him to take care of the effects I had left there.

I had to go to Lazarus. I was going to sell him the cycle—he would deal in anything. I did not care about the money anyway. But first I had to retrieve the dispatch-case, still wrapped in the cloth, which I had stowed away in the space beneath the seat of the side-car before I put Fin aboard. If it was gone, my plan for Schumann's was ruined, but I expected to find it.

Lazarus was a cheap fence, but he was crafty. He might have looked into the side-car, but he would have seen blood on the cushions and certainly would have gone no further. It was the only place I could have put and left it as things happened.

I had to get a Turkish bath. I needed a massage, after a steaming. I had to be fit and spry when I saw Schumann.

Then to my new rooms.

A disguise had to be worked out carefully, nothing in the slightest degree obvious. It must be perfect. I was sure that Schumann had a gunman in his office at all times. Schumann himself would be nervous about new customers. A personality had to be arranged that was fool-proof.

There would be a visit to the Metropolitan Museum. A printing job to be done. A cheap typewriter bought.

It would be to-morrow afternoon before I interviewed Mr. Schumann.

I picked up *El Capitán's* resplendent cape of black broadcloth, satin-lined, with a velvet collar, tasseled cords to close the neck. He would fume over losing that. It had to be got rid of. I meant to pack it in one of the cardboard boxes the clothing-salesman would bring, and send it through the post office to an imaginary name and address, from an imaginary person. The Federal government would handle it through its dead-letter department. It was safer than Lazarus, whom I first thought of.

I started to fold it up, lining out, and saw a pocket, designed for handkerchief or cigarette case, empty. But revealing. For there was the tailor's label, the date of making, and the name of the customer—the name of *El Capitán,* the Chief!

Pedro Tafoza! No address, but a find, even if he had changed it. It was not likely with the recent date, a Fifth Avenue tailor! A clew there to be followed. There was no Tafoza in the telephone books of Manhattan or the suburbs. But I could not expect too much.

THE CLOTHING CAME, with the accessories I had requested. I had to get entirely new effects, including toilet articles. It was fortunate that I was rich. The suits fitted well enough and I could not bother about alterations. I paid the man, packed the spare things and Tafoza's cloak—he

would always be *El Capitán* to me, until I was through with
him—called a cab and went to my new rooms.

I was a new man after that bath and a breakfast. Another
night's sleep would see me myself again. There was nothing in the papers, as yet, about Kate's reappearance. But
the afternoon editions would have it, the tabloids would
be busy, until I gave them something else to eclipse it. It
was under way.

Lazarus did not want to buy the motor cycle. The
dispatch case was there and I wrapped it in paper. But he
had seen the bloody cushions.

"I vouldn't gif you a nickel for it," he said. "How do I
know id ain't stolen? Vat it has been used for?"

"It's bought and paid for by me," I told him, knowing
that worried him but slightly. "It packed a man who was
hurt, but he's being looked after."

He shook his head sagely.

"Not efen as a gift, Mister."

He didn't mean that, and I knew it. I left it behind me.
I got a cheap portable typewriter and ordered my cards at
a "while-you-wait" print shop. I bought some things at a
drug store and also some address labels. When I got back I
fixed up the cloak and mailed it, on my way to the museum.
I remembered I would need a screwdriver and a tool or two,
so I stopped at a hardware store as I came back to my hotel.

Next morning I returned to the museum and secured
what I wanted there. I was bound for Nassau Street in
the early afternoon. First I rang up Schumann, and made
an appointment, giving the name, then I lunched and
attended to my disguise.

I knew the essential elements of efficient masquerade.

The main thing is to distract the attention. My plain business suit helped, of course. I did not want to look out of the ordinary so that I would be talked about, and I had to have a place to make the change where I would not be noticed. There is no place better than the lavatories at the Grand Central. They are usually busy and slight notice is taken by the attendants.

I walked through the pay-as-you-enter turnstile with a flat, thin package beneath my coat and two newspapers under my arm, smoking a pipe. In the well-fitted toilet compartment I stained my fingers with a weak solution of permanganate of potash until they looked as if I worked with acids, or perhaps smoked too many cigarettes. The newspapers I disposed of as padding under trousers and vest, not for corpulence but decidedly affecting my appearance, holding them in place with tape I had purchased.

I strengthened the permanganate, using a glass bought in a ten-cent store with a camel's hair brush I had got at the druggist's, and placed a mole, shaped like a dumb-bell, not very large, on my cheek. The purple soon faded to the right shade of brown and I added a few freckles on the back of my hands. Dioxygen would easily take all off. I was going to wear, rimmed glasses also, when I got to Nassau Street. That, with a change of speech—the barest suspicion of an accent, Slavic, not German—would suffice.

I carried the precious package under my arm when I came out, unnoticed by the busy negroes. The pipe was in my pocket.

I sent in a card to Schumann. There were two men in the outer office, that had a counter. One was there merely to see what a man wanted, take his name in, I concluded; the other, well dressed, but, to me, indefinably giving himself away, was the gunman guard. He strolled in after me to where Schumann sat in a comfortable furnished room with a safe, handed over some papers and, at a nod from Schumann, went out, leaving the door ajar.

"MR. PAVLOFF?" ASKED Schumann. I saw him take in my fingers, the freckles, the dumbbell mole. "You want to see some jewels? You understand I am only wholesale?"

He was nibbling.

"I am an artist, I said, in jewelry. Original designs only. It is on my card, with my address." He looked at it again. Then read it aloud.

There was a real Pavloff, whom I knew slightly, enough to know that he lived for art rather than from it. I do not think he dabbled in jewelry, but he had a studio—the address was authentic.

Moreover, Ivor Pavloff pursued pleasure combined with business, his patronesses, who admired his personality, at least as much as his work, being frequently his hostesses. I knew that he was in the Bahamas, would go to Florida in January and not return to New York until the early spring. Meantime he would not sublet his studio. It was shut, but there was no visible sign of its being unoccupied. His name was on a doorplate.

"I see you have no telephone," said Schumann.

"I do not like to be disturbed at my work," I answered. "I undertake only special commissions, after my designs have been accepted. If you do not care to sell to me as a craftsman, I can go elsewhere. But I came to you for a reason."

"And that was?" My nervous resentment, as I lit a cigarette and inhaled it deeply and swiftly, was effective. My reply made him take the bait in his mouth.

"I am told you have the most complete assortment of stones that I will need. I work for beauty, not for brilliancy; the Oriental method, not the Occidental. If you will please to look at this."

I gave the package to him, purposely unopened. I wanted him to handle it thoroughly. He nodded, his expression changing as he viewed the colored drawing. It was signed Ivor Pavloff, though not made by him or by me.

"That is an original, a unique design," he said, as he set it down on the flat top of his desk, poring over it.

It was unique, but hardly an original, inasmuch as I had paid one of the students who visit the museum to copy it from a case of antique Jewelry. It sent my stock up with Schumann. He was ready to swallow now.

"This central stone calls for a mine-gem," he said. "They are hard to get. Most have been recut."

"Any other cutting would not suit the design," I replied. I had been told by the curator about mine stones. Further, I knew that Mrs. Fenton's famous necklace had a mine-stone diamond in the pendant. I had little question but what it had been on the table at Schumann's, among the gems I had seen there, if it was not now in his safe.

"The design may conform to the actual size of what stone you may be able to find for me," I said. "This drawing is approximately full scale."

"I might be able to find such a stone," he said slowly. "It will take a day or so, perhaps three or four. Do you know what it will cost you?"

"That does not matter, if the price is fair. My client will

pay what the finished work is worth. I should be able to come close to the value. It is a question of the stone, Mr. Schumann, you must understand, to fit my idea."

I spoke testily, rubbing out my cigarette on his ashtray, starting another, appearing a little irritated.

"I can wait a few days," I said. "Not more than a week. My client is going to the Caribbean then. Now I have to go myself out of town for two or three days, but a letter will reach me at the address on the card, or I will call you when I return. You think there is some assurance of your finding it? I do not wish to take the time to go to many dealers."

"I will get one for you," he said. "And the price will be right." He rewrapped the sketch in his precise fashion and handed it to me. I gave him a quick, foreign bow from the hips, heels together, as a final touch.

He was hooked.

The gunman was lounging where he could see Schumann as I passed out unchallenged. I thought of Pavloff's bewilderment later to get a letter from Schumann, if Schumann had time to write it. It would be my fault if he had. I figured he would wait a day or two, for effect. He might even send down to see if Pavloff really lived there. He would find that he did, but was not at home, as I had indicated.

THE DESIGN, FOR which I had paid liberally, was on hot-pressed artist's paper, as I had stipulated. This had been covered with a *fixatif* solution by spraying, a common precaution where pastels were used, as they had been in this case, to accentuate the high-lights. So had the wrapping paper. It was not noticeable and merely gave the paper a dull glaze—but it was nicely calculated to receive fingerprints. I had plenty of Schumann's there.

There are plenty of photographers in New York who are not too prosperous. I chose an Italian who advertised portraiture and commercial work. He was idle when I arrived, glad to see some one who looked like money. But I did not look much like the man who had been to Schumann's. The padding, the glasses, the stains were gone.

I explained to him that I was an artist, a fellow artist, I emphasized. Some one had been stealing my designs. I thought I had trapped him and I wanted to make sure. He was enthusiastic over the plan I had adopted, lamenting the necessity of blowing powder on the *"bello disegno,"* the beautiful design, to bring out the prints. It did, admirably.

"They should be in the Rogues' Gallery," he said. I did not tell him I expected them to be, shortly. I said I wanted to catch my thief first and then decide what to do with him. And I waited in his grimy studio with its sample portraits of wedding-parties, of brides alone, and children in confirmation dress, while he photographed, developed, dried the films and took prints in velox for me. I bought the negatives, insisting that he undercharged me and that I took them to offset that.

Well hooked now, Schumann, on the line, being played. I had in mind the man who was going to use the landing net, the gaff. Not the police. There was too much uncertainty about them. The dispatch case might yet be "lost." There were recent, flagrant instances of records missing mysteriously from filing cases, of exhibits discovered in dicks' lockers. Once he felt himself coming in, Schumann would appeal to *El Capitán*, and his pull might break my line.

It was my zealous, very much alive editor of the tabloid, who had come so close to knowing that Richard Pemberton was in Redding's rooms the night he was killed, whom I was going to use.

The next move was to a small shop that did line-engraving and half-tones. Here I was a writer, pompous and fussy, preparing a pamphlet on Dactylography. He probably looked it up in the dictionary if he was curious enough. But he was the kind to suit me, owner of a small shop, none too busy, the smell of cheap and nasty hooch on his breath. He promised me the cuts for illustration within twenty-four hours. I told him I was a college man writing a thesis. Altogether I had him regarding me as a chump, but a customer none the less.

I had no intentions of using those cuts for printing pictures. If Billings got back from Washington he was the man I needed. He made rubber-stamps besides keys in that cover-shop of his. Otherwise I would have to go to some one else; and I wanted to cover myself as much as possible.

My tabloid journalist might want to publish finger-prints. If he did, his cuts would be made in his own engraving department. My photographer and engraver might see them. If they did, it would not do much harm. I would remain unknown.

I GOT BILLINGS'S landlady—Sara Levinsky—once more. She knew my voice before I told her it was the Kid, and he had left word that I was O.K. if I ever called up again. She expected him back that afternoon. Once more I met him, with his bulldog, in Washington Square at twilight, my line-etchings in my pocket, mounted on metal blocks. He was in good humor enough, but I thought not quite content.

"I'm glad to see you safe and sound," he told me. "My patent is granted, but"—his eyes crinkled—"the 'ell of it is,

Kid, I'm beginnin' to see a w'y to beat that burglar-proof lock of mine. Looks like I was booked to pick 'em. I don't know as any one else could, in a 'urry. I've got to work over it. And I was 'opin' to retire to that plyce of mine. Flowers an' ducks. 'Olly 'ocks an' Sweet William. Indian Runners— the ducks I mean. Now, what can I do for you?"

He chuckled, hugely, as I told him.

"You beat the Dutch, Kid. You've got brains. And they say finger-prints can't lie. These won't lie, exactly, but they'd work just the same if this bird wasn't guilty. Lor' lummy, boy, you an' me together, we could lead 'em all a merry chyse. I'll do them to-night. You can come down and get 'em yourself by twelve o'clock."

At one I was back in my rooms with the rubber stamps that held the design of Schumann's whorls and loops and islands, damning evidence in the right place. The men who had turned the trick at Fenton's had worn gloves, and Schumann had not even been there—but he couldn't get away from the fact that he had handled the dispatch case— and that fact he had overlooked. He might not have even touched it. I had not experimented with it to find out. There were going to be his prints on it now—plenty of them.

I kept the room hot until I was sweating slightly and I applied the clean rubber stamps to my forehead and then to the leather, choosing the likely spots. They might find other prints that were already on police record. If so, let the men who had left them there when they emptied out the loot at Carmel beware. My editor would see the police did not shirk. The publicity would be too great. The commissioner would take it up himself.

It was a good scheme, if I say so myself. Dipped in blood,

those same stamps might hang a man. Or similar ones. I
dropped *them* into a sewer grating later on. I discarded the
brocaded cloth and burned that in my open grate, wrapping the dispatch box carefully in tissue and then in brown
paper, sealing it for registration and special delivery. I was
going to mail it in the morning at a sub-station where there
was always a line, rushed clerks, a wicket where the one
who registered the parcel would not see my face above my
chin, doing his tedious work automatically.

The negatives were already smashed and disposed of.
Billings had melted down the engravings in his little
furnace.

The portable typewriter came into play again, first for
the label, then for the letter to the tabloid editor. He would
try, the police would try, to identify that machine, calling
experts in to trace through irregularities in type and align-
ment. There were enough of them. But I left no prints of
mine on any paper and I used my tools to take the typewriter apart, then crunched the type; and the dismantled
parts were down at Billings's next day. He got rid of them.

This is what I wrote, as it came out in the paper.

DEAR SIR:

As you will see this case belongs to Mr Fenton whose
plce was robbed not long ago. Youll find finger printz on it.
They belong to Augustus Schumann, dimond merchant and
deeler,—Nassau Street. Hes got the ice and all the stuff. Hes
just a fense. Take a look at his plcae at Carmel and see waht
you think of it. Hes got a gunman in his offis so watch out.
Hes a crook and a cheat. This is strait goods.

NEVER YOU MIND WHO.

I purposely misplaced letters, misspelled them, made lines irregular on the sheet of cheap paper from a pad and on the stamped envelope. They would make the most of all that.

I had a good appetite for my breakfast the next morning. I did not know how long I would have to wait but I could afford to, cheerfully. I only wished I could see *El Capitán's* face when he got the news. I could imagine Schumann's.

KATE'S RETURN WAS widely chronicled, with the story substantially as she had contrived it. She would be forgotten soon. But she would read about this and know who had brought off that coup. I was vain enough to want her to think well of me, but strong enough, I prayed, to keep away from her. Friendship between a man and a woman is always explosive. I knew well enough the danger of that fire.

To-day, the pink-sheeted chronicle of timely stories, the more sensational the better, has a habit of special editions, but none broke up to the time I turned in. I could imagine what was happening. They were checking up on the scoop. The case alone would verify it as probably genuine. My special delivery letter would get there ahead and they would be primed for a beat. That cost them nothing. The revenge of some squealer who had not got his share.

The editor would go straight to the commissioner. He was far from a fool. He would show the galley proofs, some pictures, his other evidence, and arrange for a simultaneous edition with the arrest, or close to it. And I was sitting in, I was tempted to hang around on Nassau Street though I knew that would be idiotic. I almost ran a fever before it broke.

Block letters across the front page:

DIAMOND MERCHANT
FOUND TO BE CROOK?

Schumann's picture was underneath, with one of the dispatch case and his finger-prints. Story on pages two and three. More pictures. Fenton's house, Gulls' Haven; Mrs. Fenton wearing the necklace. Mrs. Vanstetter in her pearls. Kate was crowded out of the pictures for lack of room, was barely mentioned in the recapitulation of the crime. They had a view of the house at Carmel.

They made the most of it and took a good deal of the glory, which was natural enough. Some of the gems were identified. Schumann protested his innocence, but—finger-prints could not lie. One "Lefty" Morton had been rounded up, captured in Schumann's office, carrying a gun. He had a record and his prints too, were on the case. Those of another known crook had been identified and a dragnet was out for him. The district attorney was holding out for enormous bail.

They hinted at the existence of a ring; and both the police and the astute editor "reserved" the name of the informer! "Reserved" was good!

The scooped papers could not ignore the story. Some compressed it, others played it up. A visiting magistrate, seated by courtesy on the bench, approved the district attorney's idea of bait By nightfall Schumann and Lefty were out. The ring had put up the money. But they were under the closest of observation. I was sure that reporters as well as detectives were watching both of them.

I wondered just what *El Capitán* would do. He could not break that evidence. Lefty had been identified by Fenton, his wife and the butler. A native, looking for glory, stated that he had seen some one strongly resembling Schumann in a waiting car near Gulls' Haven. But it was the prints that started and ended it.

Schumann's consternation must have been equaled only by the rage of *El Capitán*. Gus would be accused of carelessness and he would not know how it had happened. He had gone to his country place, it was announced, insisting that certain curious arrangements there were only for natural protection of the gems he often kept there. They found the steel curtain, the shattered glass, the broken screen, but they did not find Fin. The storm had washed out all tire tracks, if they would have considered them.

There was a trick door and an underground passage to the garage, the locking-device on the gates. The Chinese servants had been questioned and had, as usual "no savvied." For the present they were detained. It was what the editor of *To-day* must have called a "peach of a story," all the elements of sensational melodrama.

If they had only known all that had happened! The Chinese would stay dumb. Schumann and Lefty would not talk by advice of their lawyers. There was going to be a speedy trial.

It never came off.

Schumann and Lefty Morton, apparently summoned to New York the next day—there was no trace of the message—were shot in the car Lefty was driving, near Golders' Bridge. No one saw the tragedy, no one heard the shots that riddled them.

El Capitán had spoken. He was afraid of the trial, afraid

that Schumann or Lefty, or both, would weaken, or turn on him, when even the mob's pull could not save them.

Two! Four left. Tafoza, Bowerman, Mullett and Lee. Redding and Schumann dead. I had not killed, so far. Their deaths had come about through their own crimes. Lefty's also. They also were Beyond the Law!

Two!

12

A TIP-OFF

I WAS BEING shadowed. It was being done by experts, so well that I did not discover it although I was expecting something of the sort. *El Capitán* might not have pieced everything together, concerning me, but he must consider me more than merely dangerous. He would have learned from Schumann what had happened at Carmel up to the time the steel screen had lifted. There were the three dead dogs and the tied-up Chinamen, with Fin and Randall to link the connections. Probably the one thing of which he was not sure was my identity.

It was natural that he should want to clear that up, to make sure before he scotched me that I was the whole snake. For that reason alone I believe he had me watched rather than assassinated as he had Schumann and perhaps Redding. He might have ordered both these things with the sanction of his partners, but none the less, he was the suggester and, if necessary, the urger.

Even aside from that, I did not think he would want me to have a quick death. Probably Schumann and Lefty hardly knew what was going to happen when the death car overtook them, or came out from the side-road where it had lain in wait, the baby machine-guns pouring out their lead. It was all over in a few seconds. But there was too much of the jaguar in *El Capitán,* in mind as well as body, for him not to want to prolong my dying, to preface it with torture, to wipe out the memory of my having bested him, unarmed against his steel, and rescued Kate. There was an announcement in the papers that she had gone to Bermuda and I was thankful for it.

As long as I walked well-frequented streets I did not think I had much to fear, at present. That was after I had been warned of the shadow.

It was One-Wing who told me. I saw him with his stump, his begging mask of a face, and his tray of mutely offered pencils, and would have passed him until I saw by his eyes that he wanted me to stop.

My ignoring of him was discretion, not ingratitude on my part. To greet One-Wing might get him into trouble, if it did not actually identify him as a friend who, therefore, might have been helping me. *El Capitán* could make him lose his "pitch," have him generally harried by the cops. One-Wing would have learned from the cab driver that I had got away safely. But I stayed now to fumble for change, to drop a quarter in his tray and wave away a pencil.

There was nothing compromising in that. Plenty of men bestow charity because it makes them glow a bit; sometimes they do it from sheer superstition, to bring good luck or ward off bad by bribing the gods. A sort of sop to Cerberus. While I did all this, we spoke swiftly in the lip-whisper.

"You're bein' shadowed. Want to see you. Important. Not at my place. Where?"

I had to think rapidly and I gave him the address of Billings's little shop, the time for that night at ten-thirty. I felt that this was not merely curiosity on One-Wing's side to know details of what had happened to me at Mother Haggerty's. There was something in the wind. One-Wing had done a lot, was willing still to go "all the way."

I wanted Billings to be there, that I might get the benefit of his advice on what might turn up. I was needing my friends more than I had imagined in my first vainglorious idea of being a Jack-the-Giant-killer. Two of the mob were gone, but the rest were aroused and far from helpless. The peterman willingly agreed.

I thought I had lost my shadow when I went down town by the subway and just made a transfer to an express at Fourteenth Street. But I made sure as I went across town, through streets that were quiet, almost deserted. He was still with me, drifting along as if aimlessly, well enough dressed, shorter than I was, but heavy-set. I made sure of him by turning corners and then I slipped into a doorway as I got ahead with a spurt.

HE CAME AROUND the corner, hurrying a little, anxious. I stepped into sight, ostentatiously throwing away the match I had just blown out, with an audible "Damn it!" as I turned toward him.

He was going by when I stopped him for a match.

"Just used my last," I said.

He was nonplused for the moment, as I expected him to be. Didn't know what to make of it, hesitant, watching me, but automatically putting his hand in his overcoat pocket. There was a thrill of suspense. He might have his gun there and be going to use it. I did not think so. He was making up his mind as to whether I was suspicious of him, or not. The light was not very good, away from immediate lamps, but I saw a scar on one cheek and that his nose had been broken.

Then he brought out a paper pack of advertising matches. Instantly I used an old trick, credited to "Spider" Kelly, when handling unpleasant customers in the resort he set up after retiring from the ring. It is beautifully efficient.

I gave him a sharp kick on the shin as I stepped up close for the matches. Then as he yelped in anguish, his nervous system short-circuited by shock and pain, I brought my fist up from hip to jaw, caught him as he sagged, hauled him into the doorway I had used and let him slump on the steps. He looked like a Volstead Act inebriate, a victim of badly distilled wood alcohol. He was out of the way.

I was a little ahead of time. Billings's shop was dark, but I was sure he was there as I pushed the button to the buzzer that sounded behind the partition where he had his work bench. A wire was pulled, the door opened and I went in, knowing the geography of the place, back to the door in the tongue-and-groove wall.

"It's the Kid," I said.

"Right. Thought you might like to slip into a dark place. It'ud fool any one who was trailin' you. You stay back here. I'll go out in front and muck about till your man comes. What's doin', Kid?"

"I don't know till he shows," I said and sat down by the bench. Billings went out and turned on a light. I heard him clinking metal. I looked out into a melancholy space of piled-up empty boxes with high board fences about them.

I did not have long to wait. The outer door was tried, then the buzzer sounded. I heard One-Wing's voice.

"Thought I might find you in, Mr. Billings." There was

respect in it, the deference of a cadger to an independent worker high up in his profession. Billings was cordial. I had told him what One-Wing had done for me.

"Come right in," he said. "I've got your little job in back. Come and look at it." They came, the light out. One-Wing and I greeted each other in the dark. Billings pulled out a bench and we sat there, talking in low tones, the shop closed, to all appearances. Their caution affected me. It did not seem unnecessary. In my own quixotic fashion I had been rather inclined to accept the challenge as part of the game, run more risks than I had to.

"I've got some things to tell you," said One-Wing. I could tell that he was still a trifle embarrassed, awed perhaps, by being called into consultation with Billings. Flattered, but deferential. Taking care to be brief and precise. Reserving nothing.

"They're out to get you," he said. "*El Capitán* and his outfit. You've gummed their cards. I hear a lot of talk. You know how it is."

HE MEANS THE freemasonry that exists, with many degrees, between all those who live by their wits, who are outside the law. Even as, in a house like Gulls' Haven, for example, nothing goes on above or below stairs that is not commented on.

One-Wing did not get in touch with principals, but the men who worked for *El Capitán's* mob were anything but strong. They bragged in their cups and in certain phases of their drugtaking, their molls gossiped, and it leaked through to the sub-strata. One-Wing was capable of sifting it down and his capacity had been stimulated by his interest in me, through his remembrance of what Harvey Pemberton had done for him.

"It was one of the Chief's men that killed Redding," he said. "Lefty Redding must have been one of their gang. They had got so they had no use fer him an' they bumped him off. Lefty was with this guy Schumann when he took his last ride. That ties him in with that racket. The tops have always been under cover till they get discarded, looks like."

I heard Billings chuckle.

"Tell 'im what *you* know, Kid," he said. " 'Elp to clear up things. 'E may not 'ave 'ad much experience, but 'e's got brains, the Kid 'as!"

I told them of Bowerman, Mullett and Lee and my surmise as to the identity of the first two. They agreed with me. I told them of the cloak and *El Capitán's* real name— Pedro Tafoza—of how I had got rid of the garment after getting the tailor's name. Billings whistled softly.

"Kid," he said, "there's a lead. It's time we got in back of you. I can get a man to go through that tailor's dump, find his books, get Tafoza's address. He's out for you, that Wop, and the best play is to get out for him, first."

"Not you," I answered. "I'll use your advice but you've quit. I'm not dragging you back because of me."

He laughed softly in the dark.

"Quit nothin'. That lock of mine is a bloomer. I'm with you, Kid. I'm seein' you through. And One-Wing is with us, ain't you?"

"You can bank on that. This Tafoza ain't human. He'd have hang a sign on Lefty, anyways. The mob's gettin' cagy. Leery. Redding an' Schumann gone. They don't trust no one. They've got you picked out to go through, Kid. But before you put on your last clean shirt, they'll try and find out who's back of you an' make sure of who you are. What they'll do to you ain't goin' to be pretty. A third-degree'd be a picnic to it. Mr. Billings is right. We gotta get together. They got Chinks mixed up with them some way, an' those yeller devils are hell when it comes to puttin' any one across. They've got a big play on. I've put two an' two together an' I know about what they're figgerin' on. You know them big railroad scow's that come over from the Jersey side loaded with cars, under their own power, engine at the stern?"

Billings grunted assent. I knew the craft he meant. Moving slowly under their own power from the waterside terminals on the Jersey shore for New York distribution. And I guessed what he was going to divulge. It was a plan bold enough and novel enough in its daring, but not impossible. Not at this time of year with the river veiled in fog.

"They've got those cars spotted. Silk probably. I ain't sure. But they're comin' from the coast. Seattle! It'll come off round midnight to-morrow. I ain't got all the dope, but it's enough. Those racketeers blow it to their janes an' they pass it on. The molls ain't got much use fer them hopheads, only to use their kale an' jolly 'em along. Nine out of ten of 'em have got a man on the side. One of them gigolos, mostly. There's several in our crowd works the night-club racket. Eddy-the-Runt entertains in one of 'em. Clowns round. That's how I get it, see? If the bulls knew what we knew, or wanted to know it, they could clean up, easy. But what would they get out of it? Wipe the butter off their own bread, that's all.

"This Tafoza is up-to-date. They'll have launches waitin'

fer that float. Be signaled when the right car is on. They got
short-wave receivers on them launches, tuned-in to some
sendin' set they've got rigged handy on the Jersey side in
some dump. They'll jump the crew—it ain't big; loot the
car they want, an' like as not, set fire to the whole outfit out
of sheer deviltry. They'll be all hopped up. But the big news
is that the Chief is goin' to be along. I got that straight.
It's a big haul. That's what makes me think it's silk, along
with where it comes from. He don't want any slip-up like
Schumann run into."

I heard Billings chuckle again. I saw no use in telling
One-Wing about the hand I had played in that affair. There
were more vital things to talk about.

"THERE'S ANOTHER SLICK trick he played," One-Wing
went on. "They've got hold of 'Snitch' Coogan. Every one
knows he is a stool, an' he ain't goin' to last long. But the
Chief's been talkin' to him. Snitch is afraid of the dicks, he's
a born sneak, an' a stool; but he's more afraid of the Chief—
Tafoza. He knows if he crossed him he'd be crabmeat—
come in on the tide, a floater with his belly full of eels. So
Snitch is to tip the cops off to some trick that's goin' to be
pulled. There's plenty goin' on. Lots of wharf-riders. Tip
off the rum-chasers too. The river'll be free. They'll pull it
right, trust a spigotty—they're born runners. They'll have it
all laid out, and work fast. That's where the Chinks come in.
They're goin' to use 'em to unload the car. Got some Chink
connection somewhere, to handle the silk, mebbe."

And there was where a clew lay under our very noses
and we did not suspect it, plain as it was. Too plain, like the
stolen pearls Billings told me about, dropped in with the
pebbles of a small aquarium, goldfish swimming placidly

above a fortune while detectives ransacked the room, and left, disgruntled.

But here, it seemed—obviously the others thought so with me—was the chance to get *El Capitán*. To ensnare him beyond wriggling out of the net. Not the clumsy net that the police would cast, obvious, purposely so, perhaps. But to tie him up as Schumann had been, deliver him to the law, ready dressed to serve the ends of justice.

It did not entirely satisfy me. Tafoza was a monster. It would be hard to convict him of his true crimes. He would almost surely escape the supreme penalty—unless, and this I did not express, there came an opportunity of settling the supreme score.

There would almost certainly be a fight. This was no raid, officially delegated, that we were going to plan. No ordinary criminals cowed by the knowledge that their opponents were twice-armed, backed by the majesty of the will of the people. There would be a fight.

If I could meet Tafoza face to face, gun to gun, it might be that he would pay the proper penalty. In such a mood, with such a cause as mine, time, manners, customs have little to do.

My code was not that of the assassin *El Capitán*. It gave him the advantage I was willing to forego, but it should bring me my opportunity. If I rid the world of him I was not merely avenging my benefactor, protecting myself, but balancing the score for those he had often sacrificed to his selfishness, his egotism, his desire to be supreme. He had in him the soul of a Tiberius, a Nero, a Herod. But I did not pad my resolution with such quasimorality. I wanted to do this because it was my own and personal intent, based on a personal sense of equity, inspired by what I knew of him and his deeds.

"It'll take men an' money," I heard Billings say seriously. "An', if we get 'm, it'll save men and money. I can get the men. You can 'ire plenty in New York. The Kid's got the money. Let's 'ear from you, Kid. What's your plan?"

I roused myself, began to see what must be done.

"We'll need a fast launch," I said. "The best we can get hold of. We'll have to hang off the Jersey shore by the freight slips and wait for them. Board them. Get Tafoza and some witnesses. The Chinese won't do us any good. But we've got to have a starting place, and a rendezvous to take our prisoners to. It's a pirate's game. Hi-jackers, that's what we've got to be. We'll sweat them down, get the evidence, turn them over, as I did with Schumann."

One-Wing gave an exclamation, but Billings checked him.

"THE KID'S TALKIN'," the peterman said. "This is 'is particular party."

And, all the time, I was hoping that I would get my chance against the killer of my foster-father, the man who had captured Kate, who had framed me, set me beyond the law. This time he would not escape me, if I could help it. But I could not do it alone.

"I've got the money," I said. "If you'll help me."

"Count that settled," said Billings. "One-Wing said it. I'm no reformer, but this Tafoza is a butcher of 'umans. Your father—'e was all of that to you—did things for us and a lot of others that ain't been paid for. Put this bloke where 'e belongs and we're public benefactors. If he gets scragged, it serves 'im right, only the morgue's too good for 'im. I ain't much of a believer in wot they call 'ell. If a bloke don't get wot's comin' to 'im in this world, he gets off easy. We're all alike, once we get under the sod. Let 'im stew in a pen'."

Billings was right, but I could not see it then, so strongly is the idea of personal adjustment set in us. Tafoza might break prison. I had. No, I wanted him out of the way, "under the sod!"

I wanted him to know that Richard Pemberton had sent him there, and why. We are selfish in our intensest moments. This was my vendetta.

"You'd better stay 'ere, Kid," said Billings, "while we get busy. I've got a cot in the cupboard. You might get put away."

"I've got to get up town to get the money," I said.

"I've got plenty of the ready. You lie low. I know 'ow to go about this proposition. That ain't your end of it, though I said it was your party. You can pay me back. But you can't keep me out of it, any more than you could keep my dorg out of the ring, or a fight, if he was set on it. I'm in on this, Kid."

His sporting blood was up. I was not so sure of One-Wing, but I did him injustice.

"I may be a cadger," he said, "but I'm with you an' I won't dive out."

In the end they persuaded me. Aside from the money, I could not be of much use. I was a rank amateur in hiring the right recruits. I consented to take Billings's advice, and lie low until the time came for action. Here were real friends, fired with the same cause for which they had already done much.

"I'll see you get grub," Billings said. "Don't open unless

you 'ear two short rings and two long. You can take over to-morrow night. I'll be back as soon as I can."

I lay there after they had gone, looking through blank panes into a misty sky, listening to the hoots of sirens and foghorns on the river, hoping that the weather would not clear.

13

RIVER PIRATES

IT WAS A "blue" fog when we slipped down the river in a launch that was not much to look at, no modern hydroplane, but sweet enough of line and fitted with engines that could drive her better than twenty-five knots. Where Billings had got her and the gangsters with her, I neither guessed nor asked. The actual crew were hard-bitten rivermen. There was not a hophead in the outfit. They had been given their instructions and they asked no questions. They worked for me through Billings. He let them know that I was in command. Out of his underworld experience he had gathered them. No pirate ever had better men.

One-Wing was along, bereft of his begging camouflage.

"I've got both wings to work with to-night, Kid," he said. "I'm no gunman, haven't got the nerve, I reckon. I make more than most of 'em, on my own lay; but I'm in this all the way."

I believed him. Misplaced it might have been, but there was loyalty in him and Billings.

The weather was not what the latter called a pea-souper. Not the kind of fog that gathers in the Thames, on the St. Lawrence, or along the Sacramento. There was visibility, of a sort. The lights ashore were orange, they had wan reflections. A nightboat for Albany was lacking in her usual duplication in the river. It was a mist born of temperature, of cold air from the sea, battling with the warm vapors of the big city. It lay in uneven strata, it wisped.

Sometimes we ran through space that was almost clear, but it was all thickening steadily, condensing more heavily as the night wore on.

The business of the metropolis had to be maintained. Great liners and freighters might be held up outside, but the ferries plowed through the vapor with late commuters, pleasure seekers; the freights of civic commerce tried to keep schedule. Gotham had to be fed, its markets supplied. On the water the air was turbulent with strident warnings. Everything was nebulous and everything was damp. The river was a haunted place, it seemed, vague and secretive, shapes moving through it with frightful bellowings, shrill wails, hoarse grunts, ear-splitting howls, as if demons were fighting in the steam of the pit.

In the varying density of the vapor boats suddenly came into view, sometimes only portions of them, as if the fog was torn swathings of cloth. Fantastic and top-heavy grain conveyors; fussy tugs off on mysterious errands, bound for the sea; ferries shuttling, humoring the tide, dodging the rest of the traffic, small at this hour and in such weather as compared with the day, but multiplied by the mist, the raucous blasts and shrieks that rent the chilly, vaporous air.

On our left were gray cliffs where Lower Manhattan's mighty buildings reared, like telescopes half-extended, pricked with vague lights, sometimes topped with them. Earlier in the evening they had been blazing; now the workers had gone home and left the mammoth hives that seemed remote, brooding; apart from human interest. Under the river tunnels ran beneath us, trains and motors made busy traffic that never actually ceased. A land of enchantment, of wizardry, almost of unreality it seemed, a mad mirage that presently would vanish.

But it was no time for fantasies, however rapidly the imagination conjured them up. Ours was a stern-lipped, cold-eyed business. We ran down river and started to cross to the place we had agreed upon. We knew just where the big freight-scow would come out of its railroad slip. Freight trains ran on their own schedules pretty faithfully; so did their ferries.

THE WEATHER WAS thickening, but the fog was still uncertain in density, in opacity, or translucence. It was like water into which a drop of sepia has been spilled, slowly spreading itself without being stirred to an even tint. We had no trouble. We were below the landings of the river boats, the passenger ferries were lighted so that we saw them in plenty of time, and we had speed enough, power enough, to avoid almost anything. It was a handy craft, if it did need paint and smelled of bilge. It could reverse suddenly and mightily, and it could come about in an almost incredibly small area, even when running fast.

We had a horn but we did not use it. Horns were for the big, slow craft that felt their way across, a light or two barely showing until you were close on them, not for us, shuttling between them.

The man at the wheel, from whom the motor boat had been hired, could not perhaps have qualified as a seaman, but he knew his lower Hudson and he knew his craft. His tanned face was seamed with two scars, one of which puckered up an eye into a grotesque sort of perpetual wink, the other crossing his nose, which must have been almost sliced off when it happened. The fog was wet on his pilot jacket, gleaming in the light from the cabin and the binnacle, his peaked cap was tilted back cocked on a shock of brown hair.

He looked like an amiable pirate, and pirate I had no doubt he was at heart and had been more than once in practice. He was enjoying every second of this trip with its constant hazards as he flung his boat through the fog, like a taxidriver trying to beat traffic, seemingly reckless but knowing what he was about. He grinned at me. He was not going to take part in any fighting. He was to set us on board and stand by. But he was willing enough for anything.

None of them, save One-Wing and Billings, knew what I was really out for. They thought this was a hi-jacking expedition. It savored to them of a spree, a rough jest to let the other fellows do all the planning and then swoop down on them like eagles on sea-hawks, and take it away from them. They had done that sort of thing before, without question. They knew all the risks and reckoned them only as the "kick" that was in the game. Bullets or bulls, they were going to have a good time, being well paid for it.

Billings had hired them for the "boss." That was I. They took their orders from me, and would take them, unless I should show myself unfit for it, expose them to danger that was unnecessary, lose my nerve. I think they had confidence in me. I had full confidence in myself and that helped. My face must have been grim at the prospect of getting in touch with Tafoza, for I saw them gaze at it as they first came over the side and give each other little nods that were not at my expense.

The program was simple enough. My hired skipper ran the boat. He knew where he was going and until he laid us alongside the scow he was in command, as long as I had sense enough to leave him to himself. All hands knew what we were looking for, and there was small chance of our missing it. It could be positively identified when the launches that were at this moment hanging around waiting for the shore message would attach themselves to it.

They would overpower the small crew, all in the stern, all inside on a night like this, save the lookout and horn-sounder. As the tide was almost at slack they would probably allow the scow to drift while they broke the seal on the car they had spotted and set to work to transfer its contents. **"THEY TELL ME** there's Chinks with the gang," said the skipper as I stood beside him. "Look out fer knives. I sure am scared of a knife," he frankly admitted. "I've been carved twice, and I'm satisfied. You got a chance with a bullet, nowadays, even if it's through your belly, but a knife'll slice an' slash you to ribbons and then where are you? Say, I've got no use fer a gang that trains with a bunch of coolies," he added vehemently, as he swung his wheel a spoke and shaved alongside of a vague shape that had suddenly appeared in one of the patches of comparative transparency. It showed no light, it gave out no warning bellow—neither did we.

"It's a good night fer runnin'," said my captain, "if a man knows the river. We're nigh to bein' across, chief. You want me to lay her up or down river from the slip?"

"Up-tide, or what will be up-tide when she starts to flow," I said.

He nodded his head at me in approval.

"You run it," I told him. "I'm not much on navigation. That's your job. Use your own judgment."

"Right! We'll slide down on 'em. The main trick is to get on their blind side, see? They'll have two launches an' they'll run up on that hearse an' hook on both sides. Then they'll jump the crew an' git busy dumpin' the car they got spotted. We gotta let 'em git busy before we land on 'em. I reckon you know how to handle that end of it all right, all right, the way Billings played you up to us. He says you're right. That's all we want to know. Billings is O.K. Everybody knows that, even the dicks. The boys 'ud go through hell fer him, or a pal of his. I'm with you an' the boys are with you. We don't give a continental damn what your lay is. The gang likes a little excitement now an' then—an' they gotta live."

That seemed a pretty concise exposition of the gangsters' code to me. Excitement, the wherewithal to live, and an utter lack of morality.

These men had "taken a job" and they would get a kick out of it. Billings and One-Wing were motivated by gratitude, but the "boys" were working and earning money in a profession they had deliberately chosen. It might, to a certain extent, have been thrust upon them by environment, but they had to qualify to hold down the job. Once contracted for, they were "going through."

Twisted ethics and rotten philosophies, no doubt, but they constituted stubborn facts of modern existence that must be recognized, particularly by me, with my contacts.

They were a product of the times, the era of speech and jazz. I have seen much of the seamy side of life. I might be biased; but there are a lot of seams in the garments of Manhattan. And I liked this outfit. They were real. They were adventurers. Their balance of living had never been adjusted for them by those who were, supposedly, wiser than they. They themselves arranged matters from their own standpoint, circumscribed though it might be.

A man must live, as they looked at it—a man had certain things to be rightfully demanded from life and they were out to get the best of it. There was no Moses to lead them out of the wilderness of their environment. They would have kidded Moses for a "beaver." They had no religion, not the slightest belief in Heaven or hell, in punishment after death. A guy had to get things by himself. Sometimes he got the breaks, sometimes they went against him.

They were firmly convinced that all men had their price, that all men would graft if they got the chance, that most people did—government, police, lawyers, down to the men who hire snow-shovelers. Anybody would stick his hand in a pork-barrel if he could get away with it. There were examples all around them. Not a contract for the city but was salted. Graft in oil, in cement, in stocks, in prohibition. At least they went after their loot boldly. They had courage. I HAD LITTLE license to judge them. I look at life through flawed lenses.

I might easily be far better than I am. Granted certain conditions I may not contemplate, much less accept, I could be. To-night I was a hi-jacker commanding a gang of up-to-date privateersmen. I was close to my deadly enemy who was more than willing to get a chance at me. I expected also to get evidence against others of the ring.

There was a fight on our hands and my blood tingled to the prospect. I was far more excited than these businesslike chaps who were coolly overhauling their guns, heavy automatics carried in spring shoulder clips, fitted with silencers.

They handled them as nonchalantly as a plumber might inspect a wrench to be sure it was in working order before he arrived on the job. They talked in low tones, but they were not talking about their job. They did not talk shop. They were discussing whether Babe Ruth would get another three years' contract at the same figure, or more, conceding he was worth more than seventy thousand.

They talked about France having taken a boxing championship. They talked about the merits of a certain dancehall in Harlem, of a trip to Coney. Their guns would talk for them when the time came, and they were alert enough to what was going on.

All hands saw it at the same moment; the long, clumsy scow coming out of the slip slowly, under its own power, the line of cars making it look as if a section of a street had gone astray or some one had designed a new type of house boat residences. There was a white light forward, the usual green and red at starboard and port. Some one was working a melancholy horn that blatted at short intervals like a lost sheep. A sheep it was, presently to be shorn by those who sought the golden fleece.

It worked out and headed across the river on the slack, unwieldy, defenseless, looking like a modernistic drawing, the *chug-chug* of its exhaust coming clearly across the water to us; lights dim at the stern, as if they shone through smeary windows.

She was fairly plain, but they could not see us. We had no light showing at all. Everything was switched off the second we sighted her. Our engine was shut off for the time as we swung in, coming about with what way we had on, watching, trailing off her port quarter, well above her.

I went forward into the bows and was standing there endeavoring to see through a baffling patch of fog that tried to shroud the freight car scow from us, feeling how easy it would be to lose her, how hard to find her again, when I saw the two launches. Phantomlike, pale hounds let free from leash, separated but rapidly converging on their quarry—water wolves, racing in for the kill. They were without lights also, but their white hulls gave them away with the churning wakes of sea foam that V'd out behind them.

Then the thick fog-patch I had noticed seemed to spread and the three of them vanished, were swallowed up while, all about us, the mist had lifted so that it lay like dirty cotton wool shredded out ten feet above the surface of the oily, lapping water.

I heard our clutch go into gear, felt the growing tremor of her as we got under power once again. Half speed only, twice what the scow was making at that. The skipper steered by compass, but he also used his ears, standing at the wheel with his head cocked on one side.

I listened, too, not for water noises, but for the sound of guns. I imagined they would use silencers also. For the moment I had forgotten the Chinese who were said by One-Wing to be in on this racket as stevedores, though

I had wondered earlier whether the quartet I had seen at Carmel would be along. They had been dismissed by the district attorney. I knew that.

BILLINGS CAME AND stood beside me in the bow. He whispered in my ear as though he feared how sound might travel along the surface of the river.

"Skip' says they're just ahead. How about it?"

"Get going," I said, and it seemed as if every one had been listening for my order. Guns came out of the clips, they stood along the starboard rail, at bow and stern, two crouching for a leap from the top of the housing. Our brief clarity ended and we went into the thick patch that rolled like smoke all about us.

Still I could hear no sound of combat. In such weather they could get alongside without being seen, but they would make a noise looting the car, emptying it. They might be locating it first or they might have already cowed the crew, covering them while the work went on.

Then I saw, we all saw, a tenuous ray of light, such as might be thrown from a very powerful electric or carbide lantern. The beam wavered upward and seemed to signal and beckon, like a ghostly finger, pointing skyward. It was hard to explain. It came from some distance above the surface, as if from the top of one of the box cars. Vanished.

We overhauled the scow, caught at the hull with boat-hooks, lined up against her after-fenders and boarded her. All my men had shoes with soles and heels of sponge rubber, patterned to give silence and a grip. They were like so many shadows crossing from launch to scow. One launch of the looters was well forward, hardly distinguishable. They did not seem to be loading into it. They would have left a man in it, but I could see no one else.

There were two rows of cars. The one they were after seemed to be on the other side. They would have their launch close to it as soon as they had found it. Probably their radio receivers had got a message of its exact position. They were there, at work.

My men stole across the space between the sternmost cars and the engine housing. The power was off, the screw not turning, the scow drifting, but not rapidly, on the slack of the tide.

I glanced through the windows. They would, I figured, have left one or more of their men to cover the crew. Tafoza would hardly be there. If he was aboard he would be superintending the work of unloading and shipment. They would not lose any time. Once away in the fog they would let the engine crew start the scow up again, I imagined, turn in as early an alarm as they could.

The job was almost fool-proof, it seemed to me, the cleverest part of the coup the discovering which car was the right one, when it left the slip. Daring enough in daytime, but on a night like this, with the police tolled off on some fake raid—though the stool pigeon might have made it a real raid to save his own face—the affair was simple.

THE MAN AHEAD of me had stopped, stiffened. I could barely make out his bent figure as I turned from the windows with a sick horror. There were three of the freight men inside and all had been murdered, knifed; two in the back, one in the chest between his ribs. He lay on his back with his knees drawn up, the others on their faces. The weapons were plain under the lamps. So was the blood that had come from them, making a common puddle of sinister red.

They might have been covered first with guns, but they had been butchered wantonly by the Chinese.

Billings was coming aft. Big man as he was, he moved as lightly as a boxer.

"They're at it," he said. "Got the door open."

We moved forward, some between the lines of cars, to crawl beneath them, the rest of us along the narrow space by the starboard rail.

I had meant to get the drop on them, surrounding them, catching them in the act. I don't know who fired the first shot, but it boomed out in the mist with a muffled report and instantly half a dozen, a dozen others, stabbed the fog on all sides, from beneath the cars, from on top of them, along the narrow deck.

One man fell from a roof, another threw up his hands and went over the rail, falling into the cockpit of the launch that was waiting for the loot they had just begun to move. The Chinese bolted. They had no nerve for knifeplay against the shooting of my gangsters. We closed in, firing fast.

The strong ray we had seen was now turned on us. Its glare was baffled with the mist, but it revealed us and screened them. I fired and smashed the lens, hit its bearer.

Suddenly above us a roar sounded, the beat of a propeller, the roar of engines. Unseen but so close it almost grazed the cars, so it seemed to me—I could feel the wind of it—a plane came hurtling down. As it passed overhead it turned on a searchlight, a landing light that showed us all, blurred but unmistakable, looters and hijackers, the three launches, the great scow, beginning to swing with the first of the tide.

The plane banked sharply, swinging in a circle. The light was cut off.

It came on again, perilously close, a reckless master-pilot chancing his distances in that fog. It was volplaning down, headed as if it was bent upon ramming us.

Then from between the prop blades there came a little hail of tracer bullets, followed almost instantly by a burst from the Vickers gun, synchronized with the propeller. They had to point the nose of the plane at the target, but they scored before the flier kicked her up again, zooming over us, a hole torn at the waterline, the river flooding into the hull; then the plane banked, coming back.

14

SWOOPING DEATH

THAT SAVAGE ATTACK broke up the fighting on both sides. Enmity was obliterated in the necessity of getting away from the fire of that swooping ship of the air, of leaving the scow that was already careening on the starboard quarter as the water came in fast.

The attack was invisible until the plane was close upon us, then, with an increasing roar of engines, it spurted flame from the exhausts, belched leaden hail for the second time, it broke down reasoning and promoted only panic and the irresistible determination to escape from this modern dragon of destruction, manned by fiends.

The Chinese who had bolted to the launch at the starboard beam thrust it off with gabbling cries. One man leaped for it, missed and we could see him for a second or so as he clawed his way toward it, revealed by the water he clubbed up. Then man and launch were lost in the fog. Its engine started up.

Tafoza's men made for their launch on the port side, crawling under the cars. The scow's port bow was tilting, the starboard quarter lowering every moment, the decks and cars aslant. The cars must soon topple from the rails, the hull sink with its dead men in the engine room, the evidence of the broken car doors. Not much looting, if any, had actually been accomplished before we had tackled them and the plane had come racing down. Now it was coming again.

One of our side was wounded. I was myself, for that matter. I knew I had scored on the man with the light. I scumbled over another as I started for our own boat. There was nothing to do but sheer off with that snorting air-monster after us.

We gained the lifting port rail. My skipper had cast off and was holding the launch against the side with a boat-hook as the scow tipped more and more with the water in her hold.

Again there came the blast of powder-gas and lead, ripping into the scow on the starboard waterline. Then, as it lifted over us, shots came from the fuselage, all directed at my outfit assembled on the port quarter, helping the wounded man down into our launch. Its light swathed us, revealed us, showed them where to fire.

I had no doubt of that. I saw now in a flash the real reason of what had seemed a senseless attack. But that passed momentarily from my mind. The plane had gone on, as it must in its mode of flight. It would return—this time for our launch, if it could find us. Meantime, the rest of Tafoza's men were making for their craft, those already in it shouting to the rest, yelling to shove off, demoralized, unable as yet to guess any definite reason for the attack, believing themselves betrayed.

It sheered off, with one man, who had been shot in the leg by one of my crew, cursing at them as he limped forward, supporting himself by the slanting sides of box-cars.

There came a violent lurch and a crash as the angle became too great and the wheels left the rails, their flanges no longer holding them. They smashed into each other, into the water.

Billings and One-Wing shouted to me to jump. They could no longer hang on to the rail of the scow with the boathooks, so high did the underbuilt side rise. When all the cars were gone it would recover level again, before it sank. I shouted back.

I had to get that man of Tafoza's. It was not humanity that prompted me. I wanted to salvage something from our attempt, to get hold of information, if not evidence, rather than to confess failure or acknowledge that, this time, Tafoza had worsted me.

THE FELLOW LAY across the rails, emptying his gun at the retreating launch. It had deserted him and he cursed them for cowards, in lurid terms. My voice broke through to him as his last shell was fired and, in a frenzy of rage and despair, he made his last gesture and flung the weapon out into the mocking fog from which came the steady *put-put* of the deserting launch.

I set my gun muzzle to the back of his neck and ordered him to get up.

"Aw, what's the use?" he snarled. "Bump me off and git though wit' it, you damned hi-jacker!"

"I'm not bumping you off," I told him. "You'll be in the water inside of a minute. Can you swim?"

"Gord, no!" He sat up. The cars were gone, the scow was settling fast. You could hear the gurgle of the eager river inside of her. He tried to get up and his leg buckled under him. He cursed his fellows again, and crumpled.

There might be some one in that dark room behind the portières

I tried to lift him and, for the first time, found myself weak. I was losing blood from a hole in my left forearm. The strength was leaking out of it, and me, if I didn't get the bleeding stopped pretty soon. But I got him by the collar, pocketing my gun, and managed to half drag him to the side, while he helped himself with elbows and his sound knee.

The damned plane was on its circling swing again. Its searchlight was probing the fog. It dared not fly too low and the ray was feeble by the time it reached the water. But if they got in one fair burst on our launch we were gone.

Now the two decks were almost level, the scow would be awash in a few minutes. I rolled the man aboard and followed. We shot off, jumping into full speed, churning away from the wreck, veering off from the plane. It struck water about fifty feet away, its pilot pancaking skillfully so that the floats hit evenly, skimming the surface in a

shower of spray as the ship lifted. They must have seen the
settling scow and now they would try for us. But, like the
sea eagle chasing the fishhawk, they must rise again after
every swoop and, meantime, we were plowing up river, our
sturdy engines doing their best against current and the
commencement of the ebb.

All over the river foghorns made pandemonium, but it
was more than likely that none of them knew that anything
had happened out of the ordinary. They were deafened with
the sound of their own warnings, blinded to all but their
own troubles.

"It was that damn' Snitch Coogan," said One-Wing.
"Double-crossed us."

I was binding up my arm. The wound was clean. It wasn't
going to bother me much. I was lucky to have got out so
easily, considering what had happened. And we were not
out of the woods yet. That plane was still playing tag with
us. If we once became "it," our part in the game was over.

I didn't agree with One-Wing. The police had not
yet taken to amphibian patrol planes for the river, they
were not cruising in the fog to slaughter river pirates and
hi-jackers, though they might come to it before long.

There had been the beam of light on top the cars that
were now in the ooze. It had been signaling to the plane.
The plane had answered by sinking it. Why?

Because Tafoza was in the plane, on the job to see there
was no slip-up this time, perhaps to transport part of the
loot.

And, when he saw things had gone wrong again, that
his men were being attacked, he acted with devilish clever-
ness. He had shot at neither party, but at the scow, forcing

all to make for their launches. Now he was out for ours. He might think us police, though I doubted that. What I did suspect was that he had overreached himself a little. The men on the scow did not appreciate his maneuver. He might be able to explain it, later, if he deigned to explain anything, but right now, they failed to see anything in it but menace to them, inclined to be deliberate. The fine point that he hit the scow, not them, had not seeped into them. Certainly not into the belief of the man we had aboard.

THEIR BEAM, FEEBLY shining through the vapor, was probing after us, but the chances seemed on our side, unless they found one of those clear spaces in the irregular condensation.

They found it. The light came down through a shaft of translucency where rising currents had dissipated the mist, or prevented its accumulation.

It bathed us in a pallid lambency. We could see the underside of the fuselage as they went ahead, unable to fire without sighting us through the prop' blades, unable to change their angle so precipitately.

It seemed best to hold our course. The fog was distinctly lessening, beginning to shred, to dissolve in the wind that had come in from the sea, strong enough soon to disperse it. There were many gaps in it now, rifts through which faint stars twinkled.

But we swung in closer to the shore over by the commencement of the Palisades. The fog would hold longest on that side, banked against the cliffs.

Billings acted as first-aid surgeon, using waste, and binding that with handkerchiefs. He looked up as the amphibian passed, as did the man he was attending, the one I had hauled off the sinking scow.

It was folly to be certain that I had recognized that plane, but I held a strong hunch I had seen it before, rising from the little anchorage at Gulls' Haven. Our prisoner confirmed me, shaking his fist at the ship.

"I'll hang a sign on Snitch Coogan before I git through with him," he shouted, "but I'll settle first wit' the Chief. He can't monkey wit' me, the dirty-hearted wop!"

I saw here a chance to force a card or two, insure a play.

"You think the Chief was on the plane?" I said.

"Think? I know it. He was to take some of the silk, see? He told us he'd be along to see this job wasn't fumbled like the one Shu got—"

He almost bit his tongue, halting, looking at me with swift suspicion by the hooded light. I had to keep him from thinking me a personal enemy of Tafoza, whom I did not believe he knew by name.

"You don't have to be so cagy," I said coldly. Now I recognized him as one of the men who had been at the table with Schumann at Carmel, but he had seen me only muddy, capped and goggled. He did not connect me there. "We know all about Schumann. We know about Mullett and Bowerman and Lee. It's our business. It looks like the Chief was your meat," I added carelessly.

He widened his eyes. He could not figure things out satisfactorily, and he let that go in his rage against Tafoza.

"My meat! You said it. He thinks we're all meat for him. He said if this job went wrong he'd raise hell wit' us, see? He sure did, didn't he? He was after you, too, but he didn't give a damn where we come in, or went out. Shootin' like we was all a lot of tripe. An' those lice goin' off wit' the boat an' leavin' me. I'll git even wit' the bunch. You give me the chance an' I'll show you."

"You'd better leave the Chief alone," I suggested. "He's bad medicine."

"I got the same medicine he has," said the gangster. He had cooled down now, his eyes were narrowed, glittering, dangerous, his voice a cold snarl. "That wop has gone crazy. Killing-mad. He kills Shu because he thought Shu might squeal. Mebbe he might, but Lefty wouldn't."

"He probably figured Lefty knew too much," I said, drawing a long bow in the dark. There were two shafts for it, and I watched my man's face closely. "That's why Redding was bumped off. Lefty turned that trick. Were you there when he killed Harvey Pemberton?"

I could feel Billings start slightly, control himself. The gangster gave me a look that showed his mouth like a tight line, his slitted eyes flaming in a set face.

"Who in hell are you?" he asked. "What do youse know about Harvey Pemberton? Who are you, Cull?"

I LAUGHED. I had not overshot. The game was on.

"I'm not young Pemberton, anyway. And I'm not a dick. But I know a few things. Your Chief isn't as smart as he thinks he is and makes you all believe. There are always leaks. I know he killed Harvey Pemberton, and I know that the Kid is looking to get even ever since he got out of Sing Sing. The Chief knows that too. Maybe the Kid'll get him. I'm out for the Chief myself, in a way. I let him do the work, and then figured to cop the loot. I didn't get it, this trip. And I'll tell you now that he didn't kill Lefty because of anything to do with the Schumann job. It was because

Lefty plugged Redding. Your Chief cleans up as he goes along. He does not like any witnesses against him. That's why I asked you if you saw him croak Pemberton. You've been trailing with the wrong mob. You think it over."

He thought, not quite sanely, fired with the treachery he believed he had suffered both from *El Capitán* and the other members of the mob. It worked in him like malignant bacilli.

"I was there when he bumped off Pemberton," he said hoarsely. "Say, he had it fixed fer me not to come back from this trip, see? One way or another. Guy, if you're out to git the Chief, you let me do the job. I don't know what you figger on doin' wit' me—"

"Do you know where to get him? Do you know where he lives?" I asked.

"Not yet. I don't even know his name; but I'll get the lousy wop. Do I get the chance?"

"I've got nothing much against you," I said. "I told you I thought the Chief was your meat. I'll let you land, clear, if you tell me a few things I want to know. On top of that I'll pay you what you would have got for to-night, including your cut. Call it half a grand."

He regarded me calculatingly. The five hundred tempted him, his freedom, the chance to get even with the Chief, which he was not going to get if I could forestall him, knowing his wound would lay him up while mine was nothing that mercurochrome could not take care of.

"What do you want to know?" he asked guardedly.

"I want you to put me wise to where the Chief gets the dope on these cars and how they get the stuff through to Mullett and the rest."

He looked relieved. I was only a hi-jacker, after all.

"You're on!" he said.

Tafoza's plans extended to the Pacific Coast. He had men at San Francisco, Seattle and Vancouver who sold him shipping information. Spotters along the railroad routes, in railroad employ. It was not hard to find such men in these days when wages do not keep up with the pace of living, when the films show pictures that make weaklings envious.

The ring had a warehouse on the East Side, ostensibly owned by a junkman. There the stolen goods—save for the jewels—were taken and hidden, stowed behind the junk, disposed of in various lots, and delivered in the junkman's truck under his surface load. There was a lot of loot in the warehouse now.

I got the names of men who purchased the loot, retailers, manufacturers. It had been silk this time, to be handled through Lee. And I got a sudden light on the clew that had lain under our noses in the back room of Billings's little shop and escaped us. Now the word "silk" supplied it.

"How many places has Lee got?" I asked.

"Hi Lee? There's his swell layout on Fift' Avenue—the Kwanghai Bazaar—an' a store and warehouse in Chinatown under his own name. Big money in silk. The Chink's a fox. Some of the stuff was sold already. The Chief was takin' that in the plane. The rest was to go to the junk-shed. But it's all in the mud by now."

Hi Lee! A Chinaman. I had been a fool not to have seen through that name. It accounted for the Chinese at Carmel, and for those who had knifed the crew of the scow, made away with the launch.

I had what I wanted. At least I had Mullett and Bowerman and Hi Lee. Tafoza I reserved for myself. Now I knew that his hand had sent the bullet that killed my benefactor, knew it for certain, and resolution hardened in me. As for the others—I was not going to play it quite the same way as with Schumann.

I would give the information direct to the commissioner. He would be eager for it. The department had almost scored with Schumann, and they would be keen to follow that with a complete success. This time they would hold their men. There would be no question of losing them out on bail, whether they jumped it or suffered Schumann's and Lefty's fate.

And I would tip off my tabloid-editor friend of *To-day*. He had served me well once, if unintentionally, and he would be on top of the commissioner, to see the thing was not smothered, though I held little fear of that.

15

WAR ON THE RIVER

AT THAT, I went up on deck. Our engines had been taken from a powerful car—probably a stolen one—and they did their work well, but the tide and current reduced our speed to two-thirds for all they could do. Foam surged at our bows. The river was no longer placid under the blanket of the fog.

The wind from the sea, once it had penetrated the misty wall, was destroying it, acting as a solvent, whipping the water as it cleared the surface. Fog still held on both banks, broomed aside by the force of the air, but it could not last much longer. There was power back of the wind, a gale coming. We could see plenty of stars now above the wide lane in the center of the river where the wind swept up the Hudson, coming in blustering gusts that whined as they blew.

Others were crossing that lane, moving along it. A late boat from Connecticut ports, a random tug, a launch or two but not much else, since we had left the lower river. There was rain coming, heavy drops splattering down, promise of the downpour that was coming on the shoulders of the storm.

"Better get across," I told the skipper. There was no

telling how long the police might be kept with Snitch Coogan's tip-off. Our own wounded man was in the engine room with our captive, making light of the bullet in his arm, both smoking cigarettes amicably enough. They recognized each other as bravos whom mere accident had enlisted on opposite sides. They held no rancor. They kept to their code.

Our prisoner would never have told me what he had, revengeful as he was, if he had thought I was anything but a hi-jacker. But his job with Tafoza, his loyalty to that mob, had been automatically wiped out with what he considered their perfidy.

The skipper, still nonchalant—he had thoroughly enjoyed his night's work so far—set the wheel over and we emerged from the mist that still covered us. The lane was a risk, a gantlet to be run, and we had gone less than a third of the distance when we heard the roar of the plane, saw it against the sky, already volplaning down. We knew there were fingers ready on the handle of the Vickers, on the triggers of lighter weapons. This time they meant to make sure of us.

My outfit took it coolly, so far as action went, though they volubly cursed the plane and those in it with lurid comment. They made sure their automatics were loaded with full clips, with cartridges in the breeches, and stood ready to return the fire, if they ever got the opportunity.

By the time we got in pistol range it was likely to be all over, the launch raked, riddled, sunk, survivors struggling in the cold water with the rushing tide.

I gave order for all hands to spread out from stem to stern. We would be broadside, or almost so, when they shot, and the "pattern" of the machine gun had its limits. Most of the lead would center within a ring of fifteen feet and then they would have to rise, pass on. The less we clustered, the less would be our casualties.

That Tafoza was banking on a final desperate play to get rid of us was evident. The Connecticut boat crew and passengers must be watching him. I believed that he guessed that I was Pemberton, although I no longer resembled him and could not be given over to the police and identified with the man who had escaped from Sing Sing. I believed he had suspected that, from the moment he realized that he had an implacable enemy blocking his plans. I think he knew who I was when I met him at Mother Haggerty's. Now he was going to rid himself of me and all evidence against him.

The man was a natural butcher. To kill established his supremacy. The gangster was not far wrong: he was killing-mad. He was like a tiger that has tasted human blood and hungered for it. He was risking a good deal now. His plane was in the open. They had set their slant, rushing down to fire, clear us, soar again. They dared not change that angle. To nose down ever so little more meant a nose-dive, a crash on us or in the water, either equally disastrous.

And I held a notion that Tafoza, bloodthirsty as he was, valued his olive hide too dearly to risk too much.

ONE COULD NOT but admire the skipper. He knew who was in that plane, knew that Tafoza might well have recognized the launch. He was fully aware of the Chief's power; but he stood at the wheel with his hat cocked, his lips puckered in a soundless whistle, cool as an iced cucumber, calculating the chances. I left it to him.

The tide surging now against our beam set us down rapidly. The pilot of the plane had made his judgment. He could not alter his angle.

The skipper spun the spokes. We surged about and sped down river under the full thrust of our screw, the force of the tide and current, like a doubling hare dodging the open jaws of the greyhound at the last heartbeat.

It was a close call. I am not looking for any closer ones. The flyers dared not change their course. Death flew too close to them, waiting opportunity. They could not rake us, even get us amidships, but their metal tore away the rail, the planking, part of the stem at our bow. One man was shot to pieces, dead before he struck the water into which he toppled, sinking like a stone, staining the flow.

As they roared by, they fired at us from the cockpits and I saw the furious face of Tafoza and blazed back at him. The target was too small, the speed too great. I missed him, even as he missed me, while, close beside me, One-Wing fell as we sent futile bullets after the zooming plane.

Sudden snorts of whistling steam came from the river steamer, from a ferry that had seen, far off, the swoop of the airship, the blaze of her gun. The alarm was taken up by others, echoing and reechoing in the fog.

"Up river!" I called, kneeling beside One-Wing, but the skipper had us already headed against, or rather, athwart the tide, making for the city shore, for the fast-vanishing cliffs of mist that were still wreathing there.

Tafoza could hardly get us again. He was not trying. The plane, leveled from the dive, was climbing fast, making north, up the Hudson, a dim shape already. The water surged about our damaged bow. It was pouring in, but we had to keep going.

"We'll make it," said the skipper. It was the first time he had shown any emotion. "Damn those flying skunks, we'll make it!" It was the injury to his injured craft that upset his equanimity.

The whistles were still screaming when the boat of the river patrol came tearing up the lane. Enough of the situation was clear to them. Here was a launch, down by the head, a wounded duck making for cover. They probably placed us closely enough. We were no peaceful citizens out for a pleasure ride. They could not get the plane and they meant to overhaul us, board us and question us. They would do more than that, once they got a good look at the outfit.

They carried a quick-firer. We knew that well enough as we strove for safety, long before it barked its first command to stop. Normally we had the speed of them, but we were losing pace from the leak. None of us had the shadow of an excuse, an alibi. Most of us had been mugged and finger-printed. Billings was not. I was not, as Paul Standing, but they might find my prints in their index, for all that. It was the only weak point in my disguise.

They gained because we were traveling aslant and they had not yet swung directly after us. Their siren was blow-ing, we heard their megaphoned hail and once again their gun showed in a sputter of flame, but they could not get the range.

The rolling fog we strove to reach was only fifty yards away and now they shifted helm to come directly after us. The rain was pelting down, helping to make us a vague target. The river was capped with wave crests and we slogged through them, slowly losing freeboard.

One-Wing was dead. Tafoza had got him through the heart from above, a bullet that had entered at the collar bone and come out at the lower end of the spine. It added another tally to my score against Tafoza. It was because my foster-father had been good to One-Wing that he had come along, showing the nerve he claimed he lacked. **TOUCH AND GO,** it was, with us. Again and again the quick-firer barked and, on the last discharge, slugs thudded into our housing. No one was hurt. Some were lying down, others in the cabin. The skipper knew what he was doing. Afterward he told me that the course of the river boat helped him to gauge the shore as we limped into that welcome fog as a wounded river bird reaches the reeds.

We shut off power and turned again down stream, sneaking in under the piling of a wharf, out across an empty slip into the shelter of a second pier, hiding back of a sort of bulkhead that had an opening in it the skipper knew of, had used before.

Two men sank hooks into the wet planking and held us there.

"We gotta git at that leak," said the skipper, "an' we gotta do it quick. I got a pump, but I dassent start the engines. Bill, you rig it for hand. Hop to it. Come on, some of you guys, into the peak."

They gathered waste and rope ends, chocks of wood, mallets, flashlights, trooping forward into the tiny triangular compartment in the bow. The sound of muffled pounding came from there. In calm water, at rest, the leak was above the waterline and they could handle it.

Billings stayed with me, beside One-Wing. The two wounded were in the cabin.

One-Wing would never exhibit his melancholy grafter's visage again, hold out his cadging tray. He was through with all of that. He had come because he meant to "go all the way." Now he was at the far end of his trail.

We had to get rid of his body. I knew he could not, would not care what happened to it. He belonged to no faith, professed none. When he was through, that was the end of things. The act that buried him protected us, even as he would have wished.

We wrapped and bound him in a tarpaulin hatch-cover with weights to sink him, anchor him there under the pier. There was no other thing to do. A dismal ending enough. I said something of it to Billings, my voice hoarse and choking, insisting that from now on he stay out of my vendetta.

He laid his hand on my unwounded arm, his steely fingers sinking in.

"I'm not quittin', Kid, till we get rid of that butcher," he said. "You know what I told you. Like a bulldorg, I am, when I get my grip. I know 'ow you feel. You ain't safe, and that lady friend of yours ain't safe, while 'e's alive. 'E's out to get you."

I knew that well enough and was thankful Kate was in Bermuda. He would never have been merciful to her, but it was probable that he had never seen her. What his breed's nature would feel when he realized what she was, revolted me to consider.

"What do you aim to do, Kid?" Billings asked.

I told him, as far as Mullett, Bowerman and Lee were

concerned. He approved with one of his deep, throaty chuckles.

"That's the right ticket, Kid. Put 'em away. Hi Lee! Lumme, to think we didn't tumble to it he was a Chink!"

"Not all the Lees come from Virginia," I said. "But Tafoza is mine! I'll let him know who I am before I kill him. He suspects it now."

"Kill 'im, Kid," said Billings. "It's your right. But don't get sent up for it. Don't let your feelings get away with you. I'd 'ave been copped an' jugged long ago if I 'adn't made that my motter. 'Andle your feelings, don't let them 'andle you. Soon as we land, you cut uptown to your 'otel an' make a halibi. You may not need it, but halibis are like cush, like money, you never know when they'll come in 'andy. Call up the commish'. The guy that runs this boat 'll look out for the men who got 'urt. That 'ole you've got is clean. You can fix it in a bathroom. Use permanganate, lots of it, an' that patent red stuff of yours afterward. 'Ullo, they've fixed the bloody leak! We'll be lightin' out. You go to your 'otel an' I'll call you up before noon. I'll 'ave news for you. News of where Tafoza lives. I put a lad on that crib larst night. And, when you call on 'im, I'm going along. It won't be a one man's job. It won't be an easy joint to crack, and I know more tricks along that line than you do. We go in to bat together this inning, Kid."

HE WAS RIGHT. I was a sorry amateur compared to him when it came to calling on a man who was probably better guarded than the President.

As we sneaked out into what was left of the fog, the leak fixed, I tried to look over the board as the game now stood. There were several possibilities to be considered.

Tafoza might have recognized our launch. That did not so much matter. The skipper had thought of that, also that the police might have recognized it. He was not going to make his own landing, where a telephone might have sent bulls to pull us in, but another, rowing us ashore and then setting off again to a place he knew where the launch would run in to a covered boathouse by a water door and there be repaired, repainted, subtly altered in line and rig.

Did Tafoza know I had one of his men along? I thought not. The launch had refused to wait for him was in the fog before I tackled him. Tafoza might or might not have meant to get rid of him, as the man suspected. That also was a side issue, his personal affair and Tafoza's. It touched me only in the matter of whether Tafoza and the rest of his ring—Bowerman, Mullett and Lee—believed that all evidence was on the bottom of the river. If they did, they might rest easier.

My attack would upset them. It had enraged Tafoza, who would never be content until he had got rid of me. He would be still uncertain whether or not I was the foster-son of the man he had killed. But he would not hesitate in putting me out of the way, by gunplay, or, if he was subtle enough, by piercing the weak place in my armor.

With his pull he could get me arrested easily enough and my fingerprints might make matters very awkward. Finger-printing was not infallible, as I had demonstrated with Schumann, but I would have a hard time to wriggle out of that. Paul Standing would have to have a new set of whorls and loops manufactured for him. I had considered this, even discussed it with my friendly facial surgeon. It would take time. Even searing with acid would have tied me up longer than I wanted in the beginning. I should have been crippled when I most needed my fingers. And it would have been a clumsy camouflage. There would have to be some tedious form of skin grafting eventually. Meantime it was my one vulnerable spot, a risk I had to accept.

I fancied Mullett and Bowerman seldom, if ever, acted as principals in any actual robbery or delivery. They were master fences, as Schumann was, but I did not rank them cowards. Lee would be even more dangerous, I fancied. The Chinese they used were closer to Lee probably than the gunmen and others they employed. Bound by race and most likely by tong affiliations.

The point here was that they might decide not only to lie low but to move the loot in hand from the junk shop, out of sheer precaution. The fences would understand well enough the clever craftiness of Tafoza's shooting at and sinking the scow to separate the fighters, letting his own men get away, and then trying to send my outfit to perdition. The Chinese who had bolted would be handled by Hi Lee. The others might or might not think that Tafoza, the Chief, had played them a dirty trick, had been willing to sacrifice them. Sooner or later they would be reassured, but they might sulk.

It all came down to this, that the police commissioner must be given his information promptly—I must act against Tafoza before he got me out of the way.

We landed safely, found our car where we had left it. Billings had paid off; I had given the quarter-grand to my man. The outfit dispersed their various ways. Billings and I rode back together, the driver one of his pals. We said little.

One-Wing had been with us on the way out. Now he was
anchored in the slime.

16

DANGEROUS VISITORS

I GOT OFF near my hotel and Billings went on downtown. I had a long raincoat with me and I was not the only one to enter my place at such hours. But the clerk stopped me.

"We'd like to have you patronize our valet service, Mr. Standing," he said, respectfully enough. "You'll find it very good. Of course, we have no objections to having work done elsewhere, but—"

He had his commission in mind, of course, but my face stopped him. I was not annoyed at him, but the puzzle brought up by his suggestion that I was having clothes pressed and cleaned elsewhere cleared in a hunch.

"Mine came, did they?" I hazarded.

"Who brought them?"

"The Chinaman who used to be your valet. I let him go up as he said he had one of your keys."

"Oh, Chang!" I said casually, choosing a name at random. "Yes, that was all right. I'll send the rest of my things through the hotel, though. He didn't take any away with him?"

"I don't think so, sir. I didn't see him go out. The phone was busy and—"

I nodded to him and went up. A Chinaman who had

ostensibly brought pressed clothes to my rooms, with a key of mine! He had used a master key, of course, neither were there any clothes or any Chang. Tafoza's shadow had let him know where I lived, and he had borrowed a Chink from Lee.

I opened my door, reached in and pressed a light switch before I entered. When I did I landed with a bound in the middle of the room, gun in hand, looking round for Chang.

There were two rooms in the suite, beside the bathroom. That was at the rear, facing a deep closet. The sitting room came first; there were curtains between it and the bedroom, draped so that they could be drawn to close the arch between the two chambers. They were closed now. I was not sure how I had left them, or what a maid might have done to them, but I didn't like the look of them. There was a cord at one side that pulled them together or apart and I yanked at this, watching the dark bedroom. There was another closet in that.

On the whole I was not very nervous. Chang would use a knife, and a closet is a poor place to hide when the proposed victim is at all alert and has a gun. Nor was I very surprised to find no Chang at all, after a search that took some time to eliminate any chance of being taken from ambush. There were a good many places where a supple man might hide, if he was clever at it.

Chang had been clever. He had gone through everything I possessed and put them carefully back in the same places, but he had left a trace or two. Most men have some finicky habit. I have one, of always putting my handkerchiefs away so that the initial is at the right-hand top corner. Now the monogram was to the left. That was one thing, of many slight changes.

He had been sent there to find some proof of my identity. It was unlikely I would have any, but all men are fallible, and Tafoza believed in being thorough. I wondered if he had asked Chang to look for his cloak, whether he knew about that tailor's label. He probably had, and had given the tailor instructions to tell no one of his address. There were no labels in mine. No laundry marks on my linen. I sent them to a place that specialized in not marring sightly articles with tags or clumsy lettering. Chang had left no wiser than he came.

ALL THAT WAS past now. Tafoza had seen me on the boat. He would mean to finish me, no doubt of that, whether I turned out to be Richard Pemberton or not.

I bathed, attended to my wound properly, set my alarm and slept until ten o'clock. I had breakfast sent to my room. I was not going out of it until I heard from Billings. When I left I was not going to return before I had some settlement with Tafoza, and I was quite sure he was of the same mind. There would undoubtedly be a shadow waiting to pick me up, and this time I knew I would travel in deadly peril. I might be shot down in open daylight, on the sidewalk or in car or cab.

Yet I slept, physically tired, mentally resolved; and felt the better for it. The telephone rang at eleven. It was not Billings's voice.

But the pass-phrase was given, and the message: "Art Gallery, Public Library, noon."

It took me an hour to get there, dodging through subways, changing systems, coming up at last on Forty-Second Street close to the side entrance to the library, without mishap. I was fairly certain I had thrown off any trailer, made sure of it as I waited for an empty elevator and went up to a higher floor, coming back by the stairs.

Billings was there, looking at a big landscape. It was by an English painter of rural life, and Billings was interested in the view of a common, village houses with gardens, a pond with ducks.

"They don't 'ave Indian Runners 'ome," he said. "Them's Aylesbury's. What's the good word, Kid?"

We took a seat that commanded all entrances, and I told him what had happened.

"Right," he said. "We'll fool 'em. We're goin' up river, not as far as the 'Big House.' It's 'Astings-on-the 'Udson, where 'e lives. The 'ouse 'll be 'andy to the river. 'E'll 'ave a plyce where 'e could come down in that plane. The railroad runs along the bank there, but that wouldn't matter. I only got in touch with my man a little before eleven, and I've been busy since then. He cracked that crib easy. Walked right in, with the bulls chinnin' each other at the corner of the block. The books was in a back room in a cheesy box that 'e opened m a jiffy. Got the ledger. 'E's a bright lad. If that butcher ain't there, we'll wait until 'e comes 'ome. Did you fix the commish'?"

I nodded. I had written a brief but concise statement to that official before I breakfasted, another to the editor of *To-day*—both sent by Postal Union messengers I had summoned to the drug store from which I had telephoned on my zigzag way to the library. I dispatched both of them in cabs. That was a busy place, that drug store—three entrances, lunch counters, cheap libraries, cigar stand, toilet articles and stationery, quite eclipsing the mere sale of drugs.

It was there I felt I had lost my shadow after playing hide-and-seek with him at Times Square between the Interborough and the B.-M.-T. subways. If he had not been shaken off, he had a job on his hands watching three doors. Even if he had seen me send off my boys, he would not have dared to leave me. There were risks there, of course, but I believed the messages had got through. Billings agreed with me.

HE HAD HIS own precautions for our trip. A crosstown car, east. The Third Avenue Elevated, changing twice, the last time seeing empty platforms from where we made apparent exit and then changed our minds and reentered, taking the next train.

When we finally got off there was a small covered truck waiting that looked like a delivery wagon, though it had no name on it. We climbed in at the back and sat down on a bench as it started off.

Billings produced denim overalls, peaked caps with semicircular nickel badges stamped:

H. & M. WATER SERVICE

"I stamped those out myself," he said. "We're trouble-men. May get us in. Get the door open, anyway. If it don't work, we're out of luck. But I think it will."

So did I. Thankful again for Billings. I would never have thought of that. How I was going to get in the house was a problem I had not solved. But I meant to do it somehow. This way was the best.

"What does H. & M. stand for?" I asked.

"Search me, Kid. 'Udson & Manhattan, I suppose. Folks don't know those things. It's a better gag than being meter men. We'll drive right up in the wagon. Pal of mine owns it. It's been used before. Got a good engine under that 'ood."

We made good time. We might need that good engine under the hood to make our get-away. If I killed Tafoza, which was the purpose of this trip, Billings would be an accessory to the fact. We would both be considered murderers.

In my mind—in Billings's also, I imagined—we were merely executioners. We knew that Tafoza had killed, but it was not going to be easy to prove that to the law, to get Tafoza in its clutches. The same evidence that was, even now, I hoped, being used to ensnare Mullett, Bowerman and even the wily Hi Lee, would not necessarily touch Tafoza, known only as the Chief except to the three principals.

There was, of course, the danger that they might squeal and involve him, as there had been with Schumann. Tafoza did not know that yet. Even then they could only charge him with robbery.

He had set Lefty on to kill Redding, and then saw to it that Lefty was put out of the way. Schumann with him. The men who did that had never been traced. It was one of the murder mysteries that did not greatly work up public excitement, since all those involved were criminals.

There was the gangster who had owned up to me that he was present when Tafoza shot my foster-father. He told the truth, but whether he would tell it in court, involving himself, or whether he would be convincing, was quite another matter.

It seemed very certain that I, beyond the law, was the only one likely to mete out the proper punishment to Tafoza. Without question, he had killed many others in his career for more or less cause. So far he had escaped merited penalties. I had no more emotion toward the act I contemplated than I would in killing a mad dog or a ravening wolf.

Tafoza was undoubtedly a little mad, suffering from grandiose dementia. Killing, to him, established his supremacy. He was not fit to live. To rid the world of him was to perform a good deed. Not that I moralized about it. I looked at it much as Billings did. I had the right to kill him, and I was about to exercise that right.

I WAS GOING to give him a chance—not going to shoot him down in cold blood, as he had my benefactor. First, I was going to assure him that I was Pemberton, and then I was going to kill him, if he did not beat me to it. This was from no conscious desire for "fair play," or any wish to be sporting. I would not have given a mad dog a chance, and Tafoza was more dangerous. But one cannot deliberately shoot down a man in his tracks without warning. Not if one is sane. Nature's own law forbids it. I told Billings how I felt about it.

"I understand that," he said. "Know 'ow you feel. Just the syme, it's foolish. It ain't goin' to be any snap, Kid. We got to keep our wits about us. But if 'e gets you, I'll be busy myself. We want to keep our eyes peeled for tricks."

I thought so, too, remembering the panel in the wall at Redding's, the steel screen and other devices at Schumann's.

Now we were going to the house of the Chief himself, and it was not likely that we would find him less trickily protected. There would probably be a personal bodyguard, besides mechanical devices.

We rolled into the little town and stopped at a general store. Our driver, an Italian who answered to the name of Louie, went in to ask for the location of the house. There would be little sinister about Tafoza's outward mode of living, we imagined, and we were right. Louie came out and climbed into his seat with a grin.

"They seem to theenk thisa Tafoza is one swella guy," he said. "You wanta me to go right to the house?"

"Take us there and then park somewhere close by. We may come out in a 'urry, Louie. We may not come out at all. If we don't, you beat it. Don't call in the cops. It won't do you any good and it'll be too late."

"Ah, the cop'!" Louie spat his dislike. Of the underworld himself, the only members of the police and detective force he came in contact with were either those looking for him, or the more venial members of the force who took bribes and then shook down those whom they "protected." Louie's opinion was a widely shared one. He was not fair to the other men who were decent and honest and brave in their duty. Foxes seldom think highly of the hounds.

Louie felt that any man who was sworn in to take away the liberty of another was a poor specimen. That he was wrong never occurred to him. When a man gets to the place where he cannot excuse himself he is in a poor way. The cops were allied with evil spirits, in Louie's philosophy. They were his natural foes. He was not especially afraid of them; and he hated them.

"I steek around," he said. "I theenk you come out all right. To-day, thees ees my lucky day, my Saint Day."

That there was anything incongruous in his patron saint protecting him or his friends in whatever they might undertake, however unholy the deed might be considered by his religion, never occurred to him.

The house of Tafoza stood on the top of a hill, part of the natural river bank through which the railroad had made a cutting, the trains running between the eminence and the river. On the water several launches were moored. An amphibian plane floated free, riding to a buoy. There was a man busy inside the forward cockpit. It was not Tafoza, but a smaller, slighter man, probably the pilot. I was sure that it was Tafoza's plane, though he might not claim to own it openly.

THAT WAS LIKE him to let it ride there, close to his house. Clever to take advantage of the obvious. There were other privately owned amphibians along the river. The new generation was getting more and more air-minded every day. No doubt if the police investigated, following the action of last night, the man aboard would be able, if not to satisfy them, at least to avoid arrest. A plane still has privileges. It is not easy to identify. I wondered if any of our bullets had marked it.

There was probably a flavor of bravado in Tafoza's disposal of the amphibian. It tied up with his swaggering cocksuredness. He considered himself immune, a master mind—or had. His security must have been shaken of late. If the commissioner did his part, I had a notion that Tafoza would depart suddenly and leave the mob to hold the bag.

Two failures would not do him any good as a leader. It

would not be so easy to get his partners out on bail this time. He would always be dangerous as a rattlesnake, but he would run on occasion and he could not be feeling too easy in his mind now.

The house was well apart from any neighbor. It occupied the whole top of a knoll, a wooden structure that had been built forty or fifty years ago, with a railed-in walk on top of the roof, odds and ends of balconies tucked away. A fence ran around the entire premises. There was a sort of lawn, some forlorn and unattended garden beds, shrubbery, and several trees.

The blinds were drawn in front, but smoke drifted from two of the chimneys. I knew he was at home, as well as a hound knows the quarry is in its den. I had my gun in a shoulder clip, as did Billings. In addition, he carried a blackjack in his right-hand side pocket, a supple weapon of leather and lead.

The truck drew up, and we got out immediately, Billings carrying a toolcase in his left hand, I with a heavy wrench in mine. We had smudged up our hands, and I had a wipe of grease on my forehead. The overalls were well used. We looked sufficiently like mechanics to pass muster, but my pulses pounded a little and then settled down as we approached the wooden steps that led to a porch with jigsaw ornamentation. The house was on a brick foundation, and this was the main door. It was possible that we would be sent round to a back one, but our approach was all right, in the masterful manner of those connected with public service, and it might save time and trouble working our way up from the basement to the living quarters.

The truck turned, backed, and parked across the street.

Tafoza's house was at the end of it. Louie got out and lifted the hood, tinkering with the engine. It looked natural enough. There was no one to observe it, save those in Tafoza's house. We rang a bell, heard it, stood there with an air of assurance and authority. Billings took a canvas-covered notebook from his inside pocket, setting down his tool kit. In his quiet way he was an excellent actor, a better one than I was, as I stood ready to set my wrench inside the door if we were refused entrance.

It was my notion that Tafoza would sleep late. He was the luxurious type. But he would have given his orders about being disturbed, about strangers.

The man who opened the door looked like a weasel or a white rat. His suspicious eyes blinked with the pupils dilated from the drug he used.

Tafoza made a mistake in employing "dopes" where vigilance was needed. An addict is not dependable. This one was the type who is only alert when primed, and he had gone far along the opium path. He would have a gun in his pocket.

17

WELL GUARDED

"TAFOZA?" CHALLENGED BILLINGS, as if reading from his notebook. "We've got to take a look at your pipes, buddy. Water company. Leak in the mains. Heads in here. May have to shut off your water."

The man's beady eyes took us in, and he faltered.

"He's asleep," he said. "You can't come now."

"Got to, my lad. Want your 'ouse flooded?" That dropped "h" was the only flaw, but it passed. Billings shut his notebook with a snap, thrust it away, and advanced.

"Come on, Bill," he said over his shoulder to me.

"There's no leak here," said the man.

" 'Ow do you know? It ain't what there is, it's what there may be. We can't 'ave the whole system runnin' loose in your cellar. 'Ow do we get down to it?"

We were inside now. In a dark, high hall with steep, old-fashioned stairs to the left, a passage ending in a door, other doors on the right, the first folding ones. I saw them slide back a little, knew some one was watching us through them.

"You'll have to wait here," said the weasel-faced man.

"Don't keep us waiting long, son. What's the big idea? We ain't got all day!"

The folding doors closed again, silently. I noticed a hall stand for coats and hats, a small marble-topped stand with a telephone on it.

"I've got to see if he wants you to look at it," said the man. He was a little defiant, like a man who feels he has made a mistake that he is going to pay for.

Billings laughed boisterously.

"Then see 'im. Tell 'im it's Public Works. An' make it snappy. Who in 'ell do you think we are—burglars?"

I could hardly repress a snicker. Billings was British, but he could run a bluff.

The man went upstairs, disappeared. We could hear a clock ticking somewhere. There was a smell of simmering coffee. Something else, indefinable, suggestive, sinister. But we were inside. If we had to, we would fool with the pipes, and then insist upon Tafoza signing some sort of record. He was here.

Save for the ticking of the clock, there was utter silence. I told Billings in a lip whisper about the folding doors.

He nodded. He had seen them too.

"Dump's like a tomb," he said. "They must think we've got all day."

Suddenly the telephone rang. No one came to answer it. But it did not ring again.

Billings nudged me. "Extension upstairs, in 'is room," he whispered. "Listen in, Kid."

It was worth listening to.

"Wait a minute, please. Is this Mr. Tafoza?" A girl's voice. Then Tafoza's. My pulses leaped again to the sound of it. Billings was keeping watch.

"This is Tafoza. Hullo. That you, Meyerwitz? What is it?"

"I've got to see you, right away."

The voice had a slight Hebraic accent. It was also slightly agitated. The next few words told me who it was. Abe Meyerwitz, celebrated criminal lawyer, crooks' mouthpiece. The senior partner of the firm that had got bail for Schumann, been ready to defend him.

"You must come down town," he said. "They've got Mullett and Bowerman and Lee."

"What?"

"I told you."

"What for? What's the charge?"

"What would it be? Receiving stolen goods. The commissioner's on it. It's going to cost money. Mullett called me up. I don't know that we can make the bail. I saw the D.A., and he is altogether too smug. You've got to come down town right away."

There was a slight interval; then Tafoza's voice, smooth and specious.

"I'll be there."

He lied, I knew it. I realized as well that he would think of us in the hall, remember his extension, couple us with the alarm from down town.

LIGHT WAS SUDDENLY switched on, powerful, almost blinding. I glanced at Billings, snatching free my gun, as he got out his favorite blackjack. We had the same idea. We started for the stairs, and suddenly they became a blank, nothing but a sheer slant of wood, with a muffled click that was repeated as I tried the folding doors. They were fast locked. So were the others, including a door under the stairs that led to the basement.

We might have gone out through the front door. It

might have been locked by some connection. But we were not retreating, though we felt that we were trapped.

A voice came from somewhere overhead. I looked up. The high ceiling was plastered, decorated with ornate scroll designs along the cornice and about the boss of the pendant chandelier, originally gas, now changed to blazing electrics, powerful, unnecessary for a mere entrance.

"So," said the voice in the tones of Tafoza, unctuous and satisfied. "Public Service? This time I have you. Senor Standing! Perhaps you have another name? There will be none on your tombstone. And your big friend. It is Senor Billings, I think. *Dios,* what a pair of fools! You walk right into my house and think to get out again. It is I who will go. You have been very clever. But this time not so clever. Last night you were lucky with that cursed fog. To-day, not so lucky.

"You think to put the police on my friends? It would be wiser if you had put them on me, *amigo.* But you like the personal vengeance, *si?* And you give yourself away at last, Senor Richard Pemberton. Suppose I put the police on you? You will not find it easy to get out before they come. It is smart to change your face, but others know that can be done. And how about those finger-prints? I think you will go back to Sing Sing. Perhaps my friends go there also; but not me. I fly. Like the bird who sees the net. In the air. Perhaps I shall go to Bermuda. For I also read the papers, *amigo.* If you have any message for the lady? *Si?*"

My blood boiled. To think of Kate Wetherill in his power was unspeakable. And we seemed helpless. If we had come thirty minutes before! I was hoist, and Billings with me, by my own petard. The commissioner had acted promptly indeed. I did not think they could do much with Billings, save that they found me in his company. He had no record.

I said nothing. The less said, the better. We might be able to get away. It was evident that he meant to leave his partners in the lurch, seeing the game was up. He could hardly take all with him in the plane. They might stay to see we did not break out until it was too late. He could get the State Police quickly enough, and they would hold us.

The voice went on: "On second thoughts, *amigos,* I change my mind. I am ready to leave. So are those with me. It is always well to be prepared, and I have been prepared for quite a long time. Tafoza is not to be caught as you are, flies in a web. This house—I rent it furnished. It is well insured. You come to look after the water, you tell the fool who lets you in, and whom I forgive because now you cannot get out. Those doors are all steel, *amigos,* with wood veneer, and the locks are very good.

"Instead of water, you shall look out for fire. Si. The rest of the house will burn, well, after I am gone. You will be in hell. And I fly to a little heaven. Mother Haggerty tells me the girl is good to look at, to embrace. *Adios, señores, vayan con Dios!*"

The lights were switched off. There was no sound from overhead, where the chuckling devil was getting ready to leave. The head of the stairs was closed off by a door that descended silently.

EXPECTING SHOTS, WE attacked the doors, and found them as Tafoza had said—solid steel that resisted our tools.

I jumped for the telephone, tried to get police headquarters, and there was no connection. There were more men in the house than Tafoza and his doorkeeper, and they had destroyed the wire.

We battered uselessly at the doors until the sweat streamed from us. I do not know how long it was before a wisp of smoke came stealing through the slant of the stairs that we were now smashing, hoping to find a way to the cellar.

There was steel underneath that resisted all our efforts, though the smoke came stealing through at the sides, at the bottom, where the metal curved over a roller.

"Looks like we're cooked, Kid, or going to be," said Billings. " 'E's got us. Off in 'is plane by now. You got the others."

It was poor consolation. I could see that plane lifting, winging south, bound for Bermuda. Kate Wetherill defenseless. There were bootleggers there, men he could employ to kidnap her. He would leave no tracks in the air, on the way, or later. He would take her to Mexico.

Billings set a hand on my arm.

"Don't tyke it too 'ard, Kid."

I shook him off, and regretted the act, gripping his hand instead.

"I'm sorry I let you in for this," I said.

"We ain't done in yet," he answered.

But the silence was broken now. There was fuel crackling under our feet. The hall was growing hot. Soon the flames would break through the door. There would be an ultimate alarm, but the village fire forces would be inadequate. By the time they were properly augmented we would drop through into the blazing furnace underfoot. The steel doors sealed us in.

Tafoza was right. There would be no names on our tombstones. No stones at all. If they found any recognizable bodies they would be buried in the Potters' Field. The arrested men would talk as soon as they knew, through Meyerwitz, of Tafoza's defalcation. But we would be thought to be some of his men. And he would be well away. He would have his share of the loot close at hand, in negotiable currency.

We were both choking and coughing now, our eyes running, facing our fate.

Doomed! A matter of moments.

The smoke was wreathing in the hall. But through it we saw a light, at the head of the stairs. The steel door was lifting. I saw a creeping, crawling figure at the head of the slope that had been the steps, groping, halting.

"The lousy wop! Leavin' me to burn! Damn him!"

I knew that voice. It seemed incredible; but a drowning man will grasp at a straw, and a man about to burn is no less eager.

"Fin?" I called, half smothered. "Fin?"

"Who's that?"

"Standing! You know—at Carmel. Find out how to fix those stairs."

"You? Tafoza got you, too? I'll try."

There came the crash of glass, then a sudden furious pounding at the folding doors from within. That would be Louie. It meant that the fire was evident from the street. We did not want to get involved with the fire department any more than with the police. But it began to look as if we would have to make a mighty quick getaway, if that was possible, to avoid observation.

Tafoza would have set the fire to burn slowly until he got clear, perhaps through some tunnel that ran beneath the tracks to the beach; but it was likely there would be inflammables, even explosives, to hurry the job to a finish. **THERE WAS A** wind blowing on the river, wind from a southeaster, the gale of last night, dying down or resting. It would fan the flames in the old house to a raging conflagration in no time at all. Louie could not get at us. We had only one way out, and we took it. Fin could not find how the stairs worked.

Smoke had got to him from other sources than our hall. It rolled along the upper landings, torturing his unhealed lung. He was weak from illness and we saw him stagger, collapse. The boards under our feet were warping. There was a vermilion flick of upcurling flame, the crackle was changing to a roar. Louie no longer pounded on the steel doors. He had been driven back.

We clawed our way up the slope by the spindles of the banisters, made the landing at last, with the floor we had left a flood of flame that was flinging its fiery spray at the stairway.

Fin lay like a dead man. Whether Tafoza had forgotten him in the excited stress of his own predicament or whether he had deliberately left him behind, thinking him too ill to rescue himself, it is hard to tell. He was fiend enough for either course. Alone, Fin would not have got out. And without him we would have perished. The opened way at the head of the stairs alone gave us a chance.

My left arm had started to bleed again with that long haul hand-over-hand up the spindles, and it failed me as I tried to help lift Fin. But Billings picked him up as if he had been a child, while I ran down the hall to a window at the far end that overlooked the river, hoping for a balcony outside.

Billings followed. An explosion came below, a section of the flooring sagged and through it flame was vomited, scorching us, a blasting prelude to complete mastery. I smashed the window, smashed the frames with my gun— the wrench I had left below—and we got out on the balcony just as flames curled up from below and lapped the railing and floor.

It was quite a drop. Fin was helpless. Billings went first and I managed to let Fin down far enough for him to fall into Billings's strong arms. There were shouts and fire-sirens sounding but we were on the far side, out of sight, facing the river. I saw the amphibian lifting, fighting into the wind, banking, swept away like a leaf, but holding control, climbing, winging south.

Tafoza might not go to Bermuda. It might be merely a taunt to me to make what he believed my last moments more miserable, but he was quite capable of doing just that. I had wrecked his ring, broken up his mob and he was the kind who would help regain his own optimism, save his face to himself, by personal vengeance. I could not afford to take a chance on it.

I did not know where Kate was staying at Bermuda. Neither would he. But it was not a big place. It would be simple enough to find her. But a radio or cablegram might be delayed for lack of proper address. The Fentons might know. These things flashed through my mind as we got Fin across the road to the truck. I went to find Louie while Billings put him inside.

The local fire department was charging the hill, people
in an excited mob, some cars, a state policeman. Louie was
in a terrible state of mind, appealing to the firemen, shouting that he had friends inside. When I gripped him by the
shoulder he looked as if he had seen a ghost, eyes popping,
jaws sagging. It upset him so that I got him away without
any talk. People were beginning to look at us but just then
there was a second explosion, part of the roof shot up with
a gush of black smoke. One wall caved in.

It looked like a set fire to any one using his head. The fire
chief would certainly have his suspicions roused. It was up
to us to get out of there as unostentatiously and quickly
as possible.

LOUIE TOOK IT coolly now that we were clear. He edged
out of traffic, rolled down the hill, gaining speed. Fin was
conscious again. He was a minor problem but he had to
be disposed of. Between us the score had been evened.
His wound was my making. He had sent me to Mother
Haggerty's, now he had got us away from the fire that was
spouting like a torch on the hilltop behind us. True, he
had saved himself at the same time, but it was the effort in
our behalf that really weakened him. He had to be taken
care of.

"I know a place in Harlem," said Billings. "Colored joint
but they're all graduates. They don't ask questions. They'll
look out for you."

"Fine," said Fin faintly. "You're square-shooters. Tony
got raided," he went on to me. "His wife hid me out in
the woodshed, and the next day they came in from New
York for me and brought me here. I've had a hunch the
Chief thought I might have tipped you off about Mother

Haggerty's. I'm damn' sure of it now, the way he left me to cook. They'd kept me locked in, see. I didn't let on I knew it, stalling 'round weak-like, figuring on a getaway. That hunch of mine sure told me that dump wasn't healthy. The guy that was chinnin' wit' me forgets to lock me in when another one tells him the Chief wants him right away. They jumped when that bird whistled. So I got out. I savvied that cut-off racket to the stairs. It was always set nights. They opened it up the time I arrived and I twigged the handle. And here's the three of us, and the Chief thinks we're crisped. Gives us the edge on him."

I supposed it did but my mind was too busy figuring what I could best do to get in touch with Kate. The Fentons would not be at their Long Island place, Gulls' Haven. They had closed that after the Thanksgiving robbery.

It would be easy enough to get their town address, Fenton's clubs and office from directory and Blue Book. Too late to get him at his office. Delay meant all. Starting now, I could not get to Bermuda until long after midnight. If Tafoza went there direct—and I had to calculate on that—he would arrive at an hour when inquiries would be hard to make and would subject him to certain suspicion if Kate was missed later.

He fancied me annihilated, burned up in that private hell of his. He would take his time, lay his plans; perhaps not come to a real decision until he saw Kate. Then I knew well what his devilish appetite would prompt. By then I'd be there to protect her.

If possible I would do it without seeing her. That possibility was remote. And though I had fancied myself steeled to the prospect of never seeing, never talking to her again,

I felt the involuntary thrill in my veins as I thought of the look that would be in her eyes, the smile on her lips when she knew that I had flown to rescue her.

IF I GOT rid of Tafoza in the doing of it all, there would be no more need for vengeance for me. Redding, Schumann, Mullett, Bowerman and Lee—all were out of the way. Two dead, but not by my hand or will. Tafoza must be killed in fair fight. I saw now that the real reason why I wanted it that way was so that Kate would not see any blood on my hands that had not justly come there. I might be beyond the law, but she was not.

Fate had once more flung us together. Why not accept? Try to gain some happiness. I knew, with swift revulsion, that it was an idle fantasy. It could not be. She must not be tainted by my underworld infections. Friendship could not be denied, but it must not be physical. I must warn her, get rid of Tafoza and go my own lonely way as Paul Standing. I would eliminate those dangerous finger-prints of mine, exchange them, and then travel, go somewhere for a start alone.

We drove over side-roads for a time but we were safe enough. We grew bolder and I got Louie to let me off at a subway where the express would shoot me to Forty-second Street. I had stopped my arm's bleeding. I was going to the Library once more, to look at Blue Books, get telephone numbers. Then to Garden City, to the flying field. I could put in my calls there while the plane was being tuned up.

Tafoza's plane was armed, mine would not be. It made no difference. There was no more chance of finding Tafoza on the flight, nearly all of which would be after dark, than of discovering a needle in a haystack. He would count on the plane for his abduction of Kate, but long before he set his scheme for that, I would be there. It was going to be interesting to see his face before I killed him. He would fight, and neither of us might come out of it.

In any case I had finally resolved merely to warn Kate, and to seek out Tafoza rather than her. With him eliminated, I would leave, if I was able, without seeing her.

I imagine my face was grim as I got out of the truck.

Billings asked no questions. He wished me luck, hoped to see me soon. So did Fin and Louie. With the good wishes of those three outlaws in my ears, I, outlaw myself, dived into the subway.

18

DARING A GALE

IT WAS BLOWING half a gale at the flying field. The wind-cone stood out stiff as metal, pointing north and west.

"Dirty night for a trip," said the man to whom I applied for a plane. "Long hop or short?"

"Bermuda," I said.

The other whistled. "That's quite a contract, Mister, the way the wind is. Past hurricane weather and the equinoctials, but she's blowin' hard and holey."

"I'm paying for risks," I said. "I know one plane is on the way there now. I want to get there first. No one here who'll take me up?"

"There's more than one'll tackle it," he said. "But paying for risks don't wipe 'em out, Mister. You better see Farley."

Farley was an older man than I. He was lantern-jawed, lean all over, hard-bitten, scarred, with the light of the airman in his eyes. That light changed as I told him what I wanted. In my haste I misinterpreted it.

"They seemed to think you might not be afraid to go," I said.

"Afraid?" He laughed. "If you knew as much as I do about flying and then told me you were afraid to go over-sea in the face of this wind—it ain't half got going yet—I

wouldn't think any less of you. Flying's my business. I live
by it and I'm likely to die by it. I'll take you, if I can. It's a
three to one shot against us. It'll cost you three times the
ordinary rate."

"I'll pay double that if we come through," I said. "This
is a matter of life and death."

"More ways than one. Never mind the double rate. It'll
take me half an hour to get ready. The bus is tuned but I'm
going over her again. I don't want any automatic feeds
letting us down to-night in the sea. The waves'll be running
thirty feet before morning. You're sure you want to go?"

"Sure." I thought of something else. "I've got some telephoning to do."

"Right. Number Eleven hangar. I'll fix you with clothes.
When you get through telephoning, you make your will.
Mine's already fixed."

HE NODDED SARDONICALLY and went off, his eyes those
of a dare-devil.

As I had done vainly at the Library, I tried Fenton again.

There was a girl at the board in the aerodrome headquarters.

"If there's any answer to that call let me know," I said
as I went out.

It was beyond the glare of the aerodrome lighting. Dark
and cold, with a roaring wind overhead. I went into the
empty hangar out of the wind to put on my flying togs,
was just starting to step into the one-piece when a boy
came running.

"Your party is on the phone, sir," said the girl. "I couldn't
tell him who it was, but when I said it was the flying field
calling, he said he'd hold the wire."

It was Fenton.

"Pure luck you caught me here," he said. "Had a deal on and it hatched late. What can I do for you?"

"I want to get Kate Wetherill's address in Bermuda," I said.

"I can't give it to you, because she hasn't got one. She's on the way back, with Mrs. Fenton. Boat docks tomorrow morning at eight o'clock. I'm going to meet them. Better meet them with me, Standing."

"I'd like to, but I can't," I heard myself saying, truthfully enough.

Pure luck, Fenton called it. Kate was safe, and Tafoza off on a wild goose chase with the odds three to one against his arriving. Perhaps Luck or Fate was not through for the night. I was not going to meet Kate in the morning, but I would get in touch with her, warn her.

"I'm not going," I told my flyer. "One person I wanted to get in touch with has left Bermuda. I'll pay you for your trouble."

"I ought to pay you," he said. "I've never turned down a trip yet, but I'm just as pleased to stay on the ground to-night. The last weather report was not encouraging. Nearer five to one odds than three, I'd call it now. If that plane ahead of you gets through, it'll be lucky."

IT DID NOT get through. It was never definitely heard of again.

Broken remnants of a plane were washed ashore near Myrtle Beach, South Carolina, parts of a fuselage. An amphibian plane, battered to pieces in the December gale.

Some thought it had been engaged in the rum-running game. There were bullet marks in the keel.

Later a corpse was found and not identified. I found out, through Fin, that the Chief's pilot had certain tattoo marks that corresponded to those on the dead man. The odds had been five to one, the aviator said. But I should be better satisfied if they had found two bodies instead of one.

9 781618 276834